OTHER BOOKS BY GRAHAM SWIFT

THE SWEET-SHOP OWNER
SHUTTLECOCK
WATERLAND

LEARNING TO SWIM

AND OTHER STORIES

GRAHAM SWIFT

POSEIDON PRESS
NEW YORK

A Poseidon Press Book
Published by Pocket Books, A Division of Simon & Schuster, Inc.
Simon & Schuster Building
Rockefeller Center
1230 Avenue of the Americas
New York, New York 10020
This book was originally published in Great Britain
in 1982 by London Magazine Editions.

Designed by Irving Perkins Associates
Manufactured in the United States of America
1 3 5 7 9 10 8 6 4 2

Library of Congress Cataloging in Publication Data

Swift, Graham, date.
Learning to swim and other stories.
Reprint. Originally published: London: London
Magazine Editions, 1982.

I. Title.
PR6069.W47L4 1985 823'.914 84-25467
ISBN 0-671-54613-9

ACKNOWLEDGMENTS

The stories in this collection first appeared as follows: "Seraglio," "Hoffmeier's Antelope," "The Hypochondriac," and "Hotel" in the *London Magazine*; "Gabor" and "The Son" in *Punch*; "Learning to Swim" in *New Stories* 3 and "Cliffedge" in *New Stories* 5; "The Watch" in *Firebird* 1; "Chemistry" in *Winter's Tales* 27; and as a broadcast on BBC Radio 3. "The Hypochondriac" has also appeared in *Formations* (University of Wisconsin Press).

CONTENTS

LEARNING TO SWIM

Mrs. Singleton had three times thought of leaving her husband. The first time was before they were married, on a charter plane coming back from a holiday in Greece. They were students who had just graduated. They had rucksacks and faded jeans. In Greece they had stayed part of the time by a beach on an island. The island was dry and rocky with great grey and vermilion coloured rocks and when you lay on the beach it seemed that you too became a hot, basking rock. Behind the beach there were eucalyptus trees like dry, leafy bones, old men with mules and gold teeth, a fragrance of thyme, and a café with melon seeds on the floor and a jukebox which played bouzouki music and songs by Cliff Richard. All this Mr. Singleton failed to appreciate. He'd only liked the milk-warm, clear blue sea, in which he'd stayed most of the time as if afraid of foreign soil. On the plane she'd thought: He hadn't enjoyed the holiday, hadn't liked Greece at all. All that sunshine. Then she'd thought she ought not to marry him.

Though she had, a year later.

The second time was about a year after Mr. Singleton, who was a civil engineer, had begun his first big job. He became a junior partner in a firm with a growing reputation. She ought to have been pleased by this. It brought money and comfort; it enabled them to move to a house with a large garden, to live well, to think about raising a family. They spent weekends in country hotels. But Mr. Singleton seemed untouched by this. He became withdrawn and incommunicative. He went to his work austere-faced. She thought: He likes his bridges and tunnels better than me.

The third time, which was really a phase, not a single moment, was when she began to calculate how often Mr. Singleton made love to her. When she started this it was about once every fortnight on average. Then it became every three weeks. The interval had been widening for some time. This was not a predicament Mrs. Singleton viewed selfishly. Love-making had been a problem before, in their earliest days together, which, thanks to her patience and initiative, had been overcome. It was Mr. Singleton's unhappiness, not her own, that she saw in their present plight. He was distrustful of happiness as some people fear heights or open spaces. She would reassure him, encourage him again. But the averages seemed to defy her personal effort: once every three weeks, once every month . . . She thought: Things go back to as they were.

But then, by sheer chance, she became pregnant.

Now she lay on her back, eyes closed, on the coarse sand of the beach in Cornwall. It was hot and, if she opened her eyes, the sky was clear blue. This and the previous summer had been fine enough to make her husband's refusal to go abroad for holidays tolerable. If you kept your eyes closed it could be Greece or Italy or Ibiza. She wore a chocolate-brown bikini, sun-glasses, and her skin, which seldom suffered from sunburn, was already beginning to tan. She let her arms trail idly by her side, scooping up little handfuls of sand. If she turned her head to the right and looked towards the sea she could see Mr. Singleton and their son Paul standing in the shallow water. Mr. Singleton was teaching Paul to swim. "Kick!" he was saying. From here, against the gentle waves, they looked like no more than two rippling silhouettes.

"Kick!" said Mr. Singleton, "Kick!" He was like a punisher, administering lashes.

She turned her head away to face upwards. If you shut your eyes you could imagine you were the only one on the beach; if you held them shut you could be part of the beach. Mrs. Singleton imagined that in order to acquire a tan you had to let the sun make love to you.

She dug her heels in the sand and smiled involuntarily.

When she was a thin, flat-chested, studious girl in a grey school uniform Mrs. Singleton had assuaged her fear and desperation about sex with fantasies which took away from men the brute physicality she expected of them. All her lovers would be artists. Poets would write poems to her, composers would dedicate their works to her. She would even pose, naked and immaculate, for painters, who having committed her true, her eternal form to canvas, would make love to her in an impalpable, ethereal way, under the power of which her bodily and temporal self would melt away, perhaps for ever. These fantasies (for she had never entirely renounced them) had crystallized for her in the image of a sculptor, who from a cold intractable piece of stone would fashion her very essence—which would be vibrant and full of sunlight, like the statues they had seen in Greece.

At university she had worked on the assumption that all men lusted uncontrollably and insatiably after women. She had not yet encountered a man who, whilst prone to the usual instincts, possessing moreover a magnificent body with which to fulfil them, yet had scruples about doing so, seemed ashamed of his own capacities. It did not matter that Mr. Singleton was reading engineering, was scarcely artistic at all, or that his powerful physique was unlike the nebulous creatures of her dreams. She found she loved this solid man-flesh. Mrs. Singleton had thought she was the shy, inexperienced, timid girl. Overnight she discovered that she wasn't this at all. He wore tough denim shirts, spoke and smiled very little and had a way of standing very straight and upright as if he didn't need any help from anyone. She had to educate him into moments of passion, of self-forgetfulness which made her glow with her own achievement. She was happy because she had not thought she was happy and she believed she could make someone else happy. At the university girls were starting to wear jeans, record-players played the Rolling Stones and in the hush of the Modern Languages Library she read Leopardi and Verlaine. She seemed to float with confidence in a swirling, buoyant element she had never suspected would be her own.

"Kick!" she heard again from the water.

Mr. Singleton had twice thought of leaving his wife. Once was after a symphony concert they had gone to in London when they had not known each other very long and she still tried to get him to read books, to listen to music, to take an interest in art. She would buy concert or theatre tickets, and he had to seem pleased. At this concert a visiting orchestra was playing some titanic, large-scale work by a late nineteenth-century composer. A note in the programme said it represented the triumph of life over death. He had sat on his plush seat amidst the swirling barrage of sound. He had no idea what he had to do with it or the triumph of life over death. He had thought the same thought about the rapt girl on his left, the future Mrs. Singleton, who now and then bobbed, swayed or rose in her seat as if the music physically lifted her. There were at least seventy musicians on the platform. As the piece worked to its final crescendo the conductor, whose arms were flailing frantically so that his white shirt back appeared under his flying tails, looked so absurd Mr. Singleton thought he would laugh. When the music stopped and was immediately supplanted by wild cheering and clapping he thought the world had gone mad. He had struck his own hands together so as to appear to be sharing the ecstasy. Then, as they filed out, he had almost wept because he felt like an insect. He even thought she had arranged the whole business so as to humiliate him.

He thought he would not marry her.

The second time was after they had been married some years. He was one of a team of engineers working on a suspension bridge over an estuary in Ireland. They took it in turns to stay on the site and to inspect the construction work personally. Once he had to go to the very top of one of the two piers of the bridge to examine work on the bearings and housing for the main overhead cables. A lift ran up between the twin towers of the pier amidst a network of scaffolding and power cables to where a working platform was positioned. The engineer, with the supervisor and the foreman, had only to stay on the platform from where all the main features of construction were visible. The men at work on the upper sections of the towers, specialists in their trade, earning up to two hundred pounds a week—who balanced on precarious cat-walks and walked along exposed reinforcing girders—often jibed at the engineers who never left the platform. He thought he would show them. He walked out on to one of the cat-walks on the outer face of the pier where they were fitting huge grip-bolts. This was quite safe if you held on to the rails but still took some nerve. He wore a check cheesecloth shirt and his white safety helmet. It was a grey, humid August day. The cat-walk hung over greyness. The water of the estuary was the colour of dead fish. A dredger was chugging near the base of the pier. He thought, I could swim the estuary; but there is a bridge. Below him the yellow helmets of workers moved over the girders for the roadway like beetles. He took his hands from the rail. He wasn't at all afraid. He had been away from his wife all week. He thought: She knows nothing of this. If he were to step out now into the grey air he would be quite by himself, no harm would come to him...

Now Mr. Singleton stood in the water, teaching his son to swim. They were doing the water-wings exercise. The boy wore a pair of water-wings, red underneath, yellow on top, which ballooned up under his arms and chin. With this to support him, he would splutter and splash towards his father who stood facing him some feet away. After a while at this they would try the same procedure, his father moving a little nearer, but without the water-wings, and this the boy dreaded. "Kick!" said Mr. Singleton. "Use your legs!" He watched his son draw painfully towards him. The boy had not yet grasped that the body naturally floated and that if you added to this certain mechanical effects, you swam. He thought that in order to swim you had to make as much frantic movement as possible. As he struggled towards Mr. Singleton his head, which was too high out of the water, jerked messily from side to side, and his eyes which were half closed swivelled in every direction but straight ahead. "Towards me!" shouted Mr. Singleton. He held out his arms in front of him for Paul to grasp. As his son was on the point of clutching them he would step back a little, pulling his hands away, in the hope that the last desperate lunge to reach his father might really teach the boy the art of propelling himself in water. But he sometimes wondered if this were his only motive.

"Good boy. Now again."

At school Mr. Singleton had been an excellent swimmer. He had won various school titles, broken numerous records and competed successfully in ASA championships. There was a period between the ages of about thirteen and seventeen which he remembered as the happiest in his life. It wasn't the medals and trophies that made him glad, but the knowledge that he didn't have to bother about anything else. Swimming vindicated him.

He would get up every morning at six and train for two hours in the baths, and again before lunch; and when he fell asleep, exhausted, in French and English periods in the afternoon, he didn't have to bother about the indignation of the masters—lank, ill-conditioned creatures—for he had his excuse. He didn't have to bother about the physics teacher who complained to the headmaster that he would never get the exam results he needed if he didn't cut down his swimming, for the headmaster (who was an advocate of sport) came to his aid and told the physics teacher not to interfere with a boy who was a credit to the school. Nor did he have to bother about a host of other things which were supposed to be going on inside him, which made the question of what to do in the evening, at week-ends, fraught and tantalizing, which drove other boys to moodiness and recklessness. For once in the cool water of the baths, his arms reaching, his eyes fixed on the blue marker line on the bottom, his ears full so that he could hear nothing around him, he would feel quite by himself, quite sufficient. At the end of races, when for one brief instant he clung panting alone like a survivor to the finishing rail which his rivals had yet to touch, he felt an infinite peace. He went to bed early, slept soundly, kept to his training regimen; and he enjoyed this Spartan purity which disdained pleasure and disorder. Some of his school mates mocked him—for not going to dances on Saturdays or to pubs, under age, or the Expresso after school. But he did not mind. He didn't need them. He knew they were weak. None of them could hold out, depend on themselves, spurn comfort if they had to. Some of them would go under in life. And none of them could cleave the water as he did or possessed a hard, stream-lined, perfectly tuned body as he did.

Then, when he was nearly seventeen all this changed. His father, who was an engineer, though proud of his son's trophies, suddenly pressed him to different forms of success. The headmaster no longer shielded him from the physics master. He said:

"You can't swim into your future." Out of spite perhaps or an odd consistency of self-denial, he dropped swimming altogether rather than cut it down. For a year and a half he worked at his maths and physics with the same single-mindedness with which he had perfected his sport. He knew about mechanics and engineering because he knew how to make his body move through water. His work was not merely competent but good. He got to university where he might have had the leisure, if he wished, to resume his swimming. But he did not. Two years are a long gap in a swimmer's training; two years when you are near your peak can mean you will never get back to your true form. Sometimes he went for a dip in the university pool and swam slowly up and down amongst practising members of the university team, whom perhaps he could still have beaten, as a kind of relief.

Often, Mr. Singleton dreamt about swimming. He would be moving through vast expanses of water, an ocean. As he moved it did not require any effort at all. Sometimes he would go for long distances under water, but he did not have to bother about breathing. The water would be silvery-grey. And as always it seemed that as he swam he was really trying to get beyond the water, to put it behind him, as if it were a veil he were parting and he would emerge on the other side of it at last, on to some pristine shore, where he would step where no one else had stepped before.

When he made love to his wife her body got in the way; he wanted to swim through her.

Mrs. Singleton raised herself, pushed her sun-glasses up over her dark hair and sat with her arms stretched straight behind her back. A trickle of sweat ran between her breasts. They had developed to a good size since her schoolgirl days. Her skinniness in youth had stood her in good stead against the filling out of middle age, and her body was probably more mellow, more lithe and better proportioned now than it had ever been. She looked at Paul and Mr. Singleton half immersed in the shallows. It seemed to her that her husband was the real boy, standing stubbornly upright with his hands before him, and that Paul was some toy being pulled and swung relentlessly around him and towards him as though on some string. They had seen her sit up. Her husband waved, holding the boy's hand, as though for the two of them. Paul did not wave; he seemed more concerned with the water in his eyes. Mrs. Singleton did not wave back. She would have done if her son had waved. When they had left for their holiday Mr. Singleton had said to Paul, "You'll learn to swim this time. In salt water, you know, it's easier." Mrs. Singleton hoped her son wouldn't swim; so that she could wrap him, still, in the big yellow towel when he came out, rub him dry and warm, and watch her husband stand apart, his hands empty.

She watched Mr. Singleton drop his arm back to his side. "If you wouldn't splash it wouldn't go in your eyes," she just caught him say.

The night before, in their hotel room, they had argued. They always argued about half way through their holidays. It was symbolic, perhaps, of that first trip to Greece, when he had somehow refused to enjoy himself. They had to incur injuries so that they could then appreciate their leisure, like convalescents. For the first four days or so of their holiday Mr. Singleton would tend to be moody, on edge. He would excuse this as "winding down," the not-to-be-hurried process of dispelling the pressures of work. Mrs. Singleton would be patient. On about the fifth day Mrs. Singleton would begin to suspect that the winding down would never end and indeed (which she had known all along) that it was not winding down at all—he was clinging, as to a defence, to his bridges and tunnels; and she would show her resentment. At this point Mr. Singleton would retaliate by an attack upon her indolence.

Last night he had called her "flabby." He could not mean, of course, "flabby-bodied" (she could glance down, now, at her still flat belly), though such a sensual attack, would have been simpler, almost heartening, from him. He meant "flabby of attitude." And what he meant by this, or what he wanted to mean, was that *he* was not flabby; that he worked, facing the real world, erecting great solid things on the face of the land, and that, whilst he worked, he disdained work's rewards—money, pleasure, rich food, holidays abroad—that he hadn't "gone soft," as she had done since they graduated eleven years ago, with their credentials for the future and their plane tickets to Greece. She knew this toughness of her husband was only a cover for his own failure to relax and his need to keep his distance. She knew that he found no particular virtue in his bridges and tunnels (it was the last thing he wanted to do really—build); it didn't matter if they were right or wrong, they were there, he could point to them as if it vindicated him—just as when he made his infrequent, if seismic, love to her it was not a case of enjoyment or satisfaction; he just did it.

It was hot in their hotel room. Mr. Singleton stood in his blue pyjama bottoms, feet apart, like a PT instructor.

"Flabby? What do you mean—'flabby'!?" she had said, looking daunted.

But Mrs. Singleton had the advantage whenever Mr. Singleton accused her in this way of complacency, of weakness. She knew he only did it to hurt her, and so to feel guilty, and so to feel the remorse which would release his own affection for her, his vulnerability, his own need to be loved. Mrs. Singleton was used to this process, to the tenderness that was the tenderness of successively opened and reopened wounds. And she was used to being the nurse who took care of the healing scars. For though Mr. Singleton inflicted the first blow he would always make himself more guilty than he made her suffer, and Mrs. Singleton, though in pain herself, could not resist wanting to clasp and cherish her husband, wanting to wrap him up safe when his own weakness and submissiveness showed and his body became liquid and soft against her; could not resist the old spur that her husband was unhappy and it was for her to make him happy. Mr. Singleton was extraordinarily lovable when he was guilty. She would even have yielded indefinitely, foregoing her own grievance, to this extreme of comforting him for the pain he caused her, had she not discovered, in time, that this only pushed the process a stage further. Her forgiveness of him became only another level of comfort, of softness he must reject. His flesh shrank from her restoring touch.

She thought: Men go round in circles, women don't move.

She kept to her side of the hotel bed, he, with his face turned, to his. He lay like a person washed up on a beach. She reached out her hand and stroked the nape of his neck. She felt him tense. All this was a pattern.

"I'm sorry," he said, "I didn't mean—"

"It's all right, it doesn't matter."

"Doesn't it matter?" he said.

When they reached this point they were like miners racing each other for deeper and deeper seams of guilt and recrimination.

But Mrs. Singleton had given up delving to rock bottom. Perhaps it was five years ago when she had thought for the third time of leaving her husband, perhaps long before that. When they were students she'd made allowances for his constraints, his reluctances. An unhappy childhood perhaps, a strict upbringing. She thought his inhibition might be lifted by the sanction of marriage. She'd thought, after all, it would be a good thing if he married her. She had not thought what would be good for her. They stood outside Gatwick Airport, back from Greece, in the grey, wet August light. Their tanned skin had seemed to glow. Yet she'd known this mood of promise would pass. She watched him kick against contentment, against ease, against the long, glittering life-line she threw to him; and, after a while, she ceased to try to haul him in. She began to imagine again her phantom artists. She thought: People slip off the shores of the real world, back into dreams. She hadn't "gone soft," only gone back to herself. Hidden inside her like treasure there were lines of Leopardi, of Verlaine her husband would never appreciate. She thought, he doesn't need me, things run off him, like water. She even thought that her husband's neglect in making love to her was not a problem he had but a deliberate scheme to deny her. When Mrs. Singleton desired her husband she could not help herself. She would stretch back on the bed with the sheets pulled off like a blissful nude in a Modigliani. She thought this ought to gladden a man. Mr. Singleton would stand at the foot of the bed and gaze down at her. He looked like some strong, chaste knight in the legend of the Grail. He would respond to her invitation, but before he did so there would be this expression, half stern, half innocent, in his eyes. It was the sort of expression that good men in books and films are supposed to make to prostitutes. It would ensure that their love-making was marred and that afterward it would seem as if he had performed something out of duty that only she wanted. Her body would feel like stone. It was at such times, when she felt the cold, dead-weight feel of abused happiness, that Mrs. Singleton most thought she was through with Mr. Singleton. She would watch his strong, compact torso already lifting itself off the bed. She would think: He thinks he is tough, contained in himself, but he won't see what I offer him, he doesn't see how it is I who can help him.

Mrs. Singleton lay back on her striped towel on the sand. Once again she became part of the beach. The careless sounds of the seaside, of excited children's voices, of languid grownups', of wooden bats on balls, fluttered over her as she shut her eyes. She thought: It is the sort of day on which someone suddenly shouts, "Someone is drowning."

When Mrs. Singleton became pregnant she felt she had outmanoeuvred her husband. He did not really want a child (it was the last thing he wanted, Mrs. Singleton thought, a child), but he was jealous of her condition, as of some achievement he himself could attain. He was excluded from the little circle of herself and her womb, and, as though to puncture it, he began for the first time to make love to her of a kind where he took the insistent initiative. Mrs. Singleton was not greatly pleased. She seemed buoyed up by her own bigness. She noticed that her husband began to do exercises in the morning, in his underpants, press-ups, squat-jumps, as if he were getting in training for something. He was like a boy. He even became, as the term of her pregnancy drew near its end, resilient and detached again, the virile father waiting to receive the son (Mr. Singleton knew it would be a son, so did Mrs. Singleton) that she, at the appointed time, would deliver him. When the moment arrived he insisted on being present so as to prove he wasn't squeamish and to make sure he wouldn't be tricked in the transaction. Mrs. Singleton was not daunted. When the pains became frequent she wasn't at all afraid. There were big, watery lights clawing down from the ceiling of the delivery room like the lights in dentists' surgeries. She could just see her husband looking down at her. His face was white and clammy. It was his fault for wanting to be there. She had to push, as though away from him. Then she knew it was happening. She stretched back. She was a great surface of warm, splitting rock and Paul was struggling bravely up into the sunlight. She had to coax him with her cries. She felt him emerge like a trapped survivor. The doctor groped with rubber gloves. "There we are," he said. She managed to look at Mr. Singleton. She wanted suddenly to put him back inside for good where Paul had come from. With a fleeting pity she saw that this was what Mr. Singleton wanted too. His eyes were half closed. She kept hers on him. He seemed to wilt under her gaze. All his toughness and control were draining from him and she was glad. She lay back triumphant and glad. The doctor was holding Paul; but she looked, beyond, at Mr. Singleton. He was far away like an insect. She knew he couldn't hold out. He was going to faint. He was looking where her legs were spread. His eyes went out of focus. He was going to faint, keel over, right there on the spot.

Mrs. Singleton grew restless, though she lay unmoving on the beach. Wasps were buzzing close to her head, round their picnic bag. She thought that Mr. Singleton and Paul had been too long at their swimming lesson. They should come out. It never struck her, hot as she was, to get up and join her husband and son in the sea. Whenever Mrs. Singleton wanted a swim she would wait until there was an opportunity to go in by herself; then she would wade out, dip her shoulders under suddenly and paddle about contentedly, keeping her hair dry, as though she were soaking herself in a large bath. They did not bathe as a family; nor did Mrs. Singleton swim with Mr. Singleton—who now and then, too, would get up by himself and enter the sea, swim at once about fifty yards out, then cruise for long stretches, with a powerful crawl or butterfly, back and forth across the bay. When this happened Mrs. Singleton would engage her son in talk so he would not watch his father. Mrs. Singleton did not swim with Paul either. He was too old now to cradle between her knees in the very shallow water, and she was somehow afraid that while Paul splashed and kicked around her he would suddenly learn how to swim. She had this feeling that Paul would only swim while she was in the sea, too. She did not want this to happen, but it reassured her and gave her sufficient confidence to let Mr. Singleton continue his swimming lessons with Paul. These lessons were obsessive, indefatigable. Every Sunday morning at seven, when they were at home, Mr. Singleton would take Paul to the baths for yet another attempt. Part of this, of course, was that Mr. Singleton was determined that his son should swim; but it enabled him also to avoid the Sunday morning languor: extra hours in bed, leisurely love-making.

Once, in a room at college, Mr. Singleton had told Mrs. Singleton about his swimming, about his training sessions, races;

about what it felt like when you could swim really well. She had run her fingers over his long, naked back.

Mrs. Singleton sat up and rubbed sun-tan lotion on to her thighs. Down near the water's edge, Mr. Singleton was standing about waist deep, supporting Paul who, gripped by his father's hands, water wings still on, was flailing, face down, at the surface. Mr. Singleton kept saying, "No, keep still." He was trying to get Paul to hold his body straight and relaxed so he would float. But each time as Paul nearly succeeded he would panic, fearing his father would let go, and thrash wildly. When he calmed down and Mr. Singleton held him, Mrs. Singleton could see the water running off his face like tears.

Mrs. Singleton did not alarm herself at this distress of her son. It was a guarantee against Mr. Singleton's influence, an assurance that Paul was not going to swim; nor was he to be imbued with any of his father's sullen hardiness. When Mrs. Singleton saw her son suffer, it pleased her and she felt loving towards him. She felt that an invisible thread ran between her and the boy which commanded him not to swim, and she felt that Mr. Singleton knew that it was because of her that his efforts with Paul were in vain. Even now, as Mr. Singleton prepared for another attempt, the boy was looking at her smoothing the sun-tan oil on to her legs.

"Come on, Paul," said Mr. Singleton. His wet shoulders shone like metal.

When Paul was born it seemed to Mrs. Singleton that her life with her husband was dissolved, as a mirage dissolves, and that she could return again to what she was before she knew him. She let her staved-off hunger for happiness and her old suppressed dreams revive. But then they were not dreams, because they had a physical object and she knew she needed them in order to live. She did not disguise from herself what she needed. She knew that she wanted the kind of close, even erotic relationship with her son that women who have rejected their husbands have been known to have. The kind of relationship in which the son must hurt the mother, the mother the son. But she willed it, as if there would be no pain. Mrs. Singleton waited for her son to grow. She trembled when she thought of him at eighteen or twenty. When he was grown he would be slim and light and slender, like a boy even though he was a man. He would not need a strong body because all his power would be inside. He would be all fire and life in essence. He would become an artist, a sculptor. She would pose for him naked (she would keep her body trim for this), and he would sculpt her. He would hold the chisel. His hands would guide the cold metal over the stone and its blows would strike sunlight.

Mrs. Singleton thought: All the best statues they had seen in Greece seemed to have been dredged up from the sea.

She finished rubbing the lotion on to her insteps and put the cap back on the tube. As she did so she heard something that made her truly alarmed. It was Mr. Singleton saying, "That's it, that's the way! At last! Now keep it going!" She looked up. Paul was in the same position as before but he had learnt to make slower, regular motions with his limbs and his body no longer sagged in the middle. Though he still wore the water-wings he was moving, somewhat laboriously, forwards so that Mr. Singleton had to walk along with him; and at one point Mr. Singleton removed one of his hands from under the boy's ribs and simultaneously looked at his wife and smiled. His shoulders flashed. It was not a smile meant for her. She could see that. And it was not one of her husband's usual, infrequent, rather mechanical smiles. It was the smile a person makes about some joy inside, hidden and incommunicable.

"That's enough," thought Mrs. Singleton, getting to her feet, pretending not to have noticed, behind her sun-glasses, what had happened in the water. It *was* enough: They had been in the water for what seemed like an hour. He was only doing it because of their row last night, to make her feel he was not outmatched by using the reserve weapon of Paul. And, she added with relief to herself, Paul still had the water-wings and one hand to support him.

"That's enough now!" she shouted aloud, as if she were slightly, but not ill-humouredly, peeved at being neglected. "Come on in now!" She had picked up her purse as a quickly conceived ruse as she got up, and as she walked towards the water's edge she waved it above her head. "Who wants an ice-cream?"

Mr. Singleton ignored his wife. "Well done, Paul," he said. "Let's try that again."

Mrs. Singleton knew he would do this. She stood on the little ridge of sand just above where the beach, becoming fine shingle, shelved into the sea. She replaced a loose strap of her bikini over her shoulder and with a finger of each hand pulled the bottom half down over her buttocks. She stood feet apart, slightly on her toes, like a gymnast. She knew other eyes on the beach would be on her. It flattered her that she—and her husband, too—received admiring glances from those around. She thought, with relish for the irony: Perhaps they think we are happy, beautiful people. For all her girlhood diffidence, Mrs. Singleton enjoyed displaying her attractions and she liked to see other people's pleasure. When she lay sunbathing she imagined making love to all the moody, pubescent boys on holiday with their parents, with their slim waists and their quick heels.

"See if you can do it without me holding you," said Mr. Singleton. "I'll help you at first." He stooped over Paul. He looked like a mechanic making final adjustments to some prototype machine.

"Don't you want an ice-cream then, Paul?" said Mrs. Singleton. "They've got those chocolate ones."

Paul looked up. His short wet hair stood up in spikes. He looked like a prisoner offered a chance of escape, but the plastic water-wings, like some absurd pillory, kept him fixed.

Mrs. Singleton thought: He crawled out of me; now I have to lure him back with ice-cream.

"Can't you see he was getting the hang of it?" Mr. Singleton said. "If he comes out now he'll—"

"Hang of it! It was you. You were holding him all the time."

She thought: Perhaps I am hurting my son.

Mr. Singleton glared at Mrs. Singleton. He gripped Paul's shoulders. "You don't want to get out now, do you Paul?" He looked suddenly as if he really might drown Paul rather than let him come out.

Mrs. Singleton's heart raced. She wasn't good at rescues, at resuscitations. She knew this because of her life with her husband.

"Come on, you can go back in later," she said.

Paul was a hostage. She was playing for time, not wanting to harm the innocent.

She stood on the sand like a marooned woman watching for ships. The sea, in the sheltered bay, was almost flat calm. A few, glassy waves idled in but were smoothed out before they could break. On the headlands there were outcrops of scaly rocks like basking lizards. The island in Greece had been where Theseus left Ariadne. Out over the blue water, beyond the heads of bobbing swimmers, seagulls flapped like scraps of paper.

Mr. Singleton looked at Mrs. Singleton. She was a fussy mother daubed with Ambre Solaire, trying to bribe her son with silly ice-creams; though if you forgot this she was a beautiful, tanned girl, like the girls men imagine on desert islands. But then, in Mr. Singleton's dreams, there was no one else on the untouched shore he ceaselessly swam to.

He thought, If Paul could swim, then I could leave her.

Mrs. Singleton looked at her husband. She felt afraid. The water's edge was like a dividing line between them which marked off the territory in which each existed. Perhaps they could never cross over.

"Well, I'm getting the ice-creams: you'd better get out."

She turned and paced up the sand. Behind the beach was an ice-cream van painted like a fairground.

Paul Singleton looked at his mother. He thought: She is deserting me—or I am deserting her. He wanted to get out to follow her. Her feet made puffs of sand which stuck to her ankles, and you could see all her body as she strode up the beach. But he was afraid of his father and his gripping hands. And he was afraid of his mother, too. How she would wrap him, if he came out, in the big yellow towel like egg yolk, how she would want him to get close to her smooth, sticky body, like a mouth that would swallow him. He thought: The yellow towel humiliated him, his father's hands humiliated him. The water-wings humiliated him: You put them on and became a puppet. So much of life is humiliation. It was how you won love. His father was taking off the water-wings like a man unlocking a chastity belt. He said: "Now try the same, coming towards me." His father stood some feet away from him. He was a huge, straight man, like the pier of a bridge. "Try." Paul Singleton was six. He was terrified of water. Every time he entered it he had to fight down fear. His father never realized this. He thought it was simple; you said: "Only water, no need to be afraid." His father did not know what fear was; the same as he did not know what fun was. Paul Singleton hated water. He hated it in his mouth and in his eyes. He hated the chlorine smell of the swimming baths, the wet, slippery tiles, the echoing whoops and screams. He hated it when his father read to him from *The Water Babies*. It was the only story his father read, because, since he didn't know fear or fun, he was really sentimental. His mother read lots of stories. "Come on then. I'll catch you." Paul Singleton held out his arms and raised one leg. This was the worst moment. Perhaps having no help was most humiliating. If you did not swim you sank like a statue. They would drag him out, his skin streaming. His father would say: "I didn't mean . . ." But if he swam his mother would be forsaken. She would stand on the beach with chocolate ice-cream running down her arm. There was no way out; there were all these things to be afraid of and no weapons. But then, perhaps he was not afraid of his mother nor his father, nor of water, but of something else. He had felt it just now—when he'd struck out with rhythmic, reaching strokes and his feet had come off the bottom and his father's hand had slipped from under his chest: as if he had mistaken what his fear was; as if he had been unconsciously pretending, even to himself, so as to execute some plan. He lowered his chin into the water. "Come on!" said Mr. Singleton. He launched himself forward and felt the sand leave his feet and his legs wriggle like cut ropes. "There," said his father as he realized. "There!" His father stood like a man waiting to clasp a lover; there was a gleam on his face. "Towards me! Towards me!" said his father suddenly. But he kicked and struck, half in panic, half in pride, away from his father, away from the shore, away, in this strange new element that seemed all his own.

HOFFMEIER'S ANTELOPE

UNCLE WALTER HAD HIS OWN theory of the value of zoos. He would say, eyeing us all from the head of the table: "Zoos ought to make us humble. When we visit them we ought to reflect—mere humans, mere evolutionary upstarts that we are—that we shall never have the speed of the cheetah, the strength of the bear, the grace of the gazelle, the agility of the gibbon. Zoos curb our pride; they show us our inadequacies..."

Having launched on this favourite theme, he would proceed inexorably to elaborate it, cataloguing joyously the virtues of animal after animal, so that I (a precocious boy, doing "A" levels), for whom zoos were, in one sense, places of rank vulgarity—tormenting elephants with ice-cream wrappers, grinning at monkeys copulating—could not resist punctuating his raptures with the one word: "Cages."

Uncle Walter would not be daunted. He would continue his

speech, come to rest again on the refrain, "Show us our inadequacies," and, leaving us free once more to gobble his wife's rock cakes and lemon-meringue pie, lean back in his chair as if his case were beyond dispute.

My uncle was not, so far as I knew, a religious man; but sometimes, after declaiming in this almost scriptural fashion, his face would take on the serene, linear looks of a Byzantine saint. It made one forget for a moment the real uncle: pop-eyed, pale skinned, with stains of tobacco, like the ink smudges of schoolboys, on his fingers and teeth, a mouth apt to twitch and to generate more spittle than it was capable of holding—and a less defined, overall awkwardness, as if the mould of his own features somehow constricted him. Every time we visited him for Sunday tea—in that cramped front room laden with books, photos, certificates and the odd stuffed insectivore, like a Victorian parlour in which "enthusiasts" would regularly meet—he would not fail to instil in us the moral advantages of zoos. When he came at last to a halt and began to light his pipe, his wife (my Aunt Mary), a small, mousy, but not unattractive woman, would get up embarrassedly and start to remove plates.

He lived in Finchley and was deputy keeper at one of the mammal houses at the Zoo. Martyr to his work, he would leave his home at all hours for a quite different world. After twenty-five years of marriage, he treated his wife like something he was still not quite certain how to handle.

We lived in the country not far from Norwich. It was perhaps because I regarded myself as closer to nature than Uncle Walter that I felt obliged to sneer at the artifice of zoos. Near our house were some woods, vestiges of a former royal hunting forest, in which you could sometimes glimpse wild fallow deer. One year, when I was still a boy, the deer vanished. About every six weeks we used to travel down to London to see my grandparents who lived in Highgate. And the weekend would always be rounded off by a visit to my uncle, who would meet us, usually, at the Zoo, then take us home to tea.

I scorned London, for the same reason that I despised zoos and remained loyal to my rural heritage. In fact I liked animals—and couldn't deny my uncle's knowledge of them. At the same time I developed interests which were hardly likely to keep me in the countryside. I took a degree in mathematics.

It was on one of those Sundays as guests of Uncle Walter that we were first introduced to the Hoffmeier's Antelopes. There were a pair of these rare and delicate animals at the Zoo, which, just then, to the great joy of the staff (my uncle in particular) had produced a solitary issue—a female. Neither adults nor young were as yet on view to the general public but we were ushered in on a special permit.

Rufous-brown, twig-legged, no more than eighteen inches off the ground when mature, these tender creatures looked up at us with dark, melting eyes and twitching flanks as Uncle Walter enjoined us not to come too near and to make only the gentlest movements. The new-born female, trembling by its mother, was no bigger and more fragile than a puppy. They were, so Uncle Walter told us, one of a variety of kinds of tiny antelope native to the dense forests of west and central Africa. The particular species before us had been discovered and recorded as a distinct strain only in the late forties. Twenty years later a survey had declared it extinct in the wild.

We looked at these plaintive, captive survivors and were suitably moved.

"Oh, *aren't* they *sweet!*" said my mother, with a lack, perhaps, of true decorum.

"Er, notice," said Uncle Walter, crouching inside the pen, "the minute horns, the large eyes—nocturnal animals of course—the legs, no thicker, beneath the joint, than my finger, but capable of leaps of up to ten feet."

He wiped the spit from the corner of his mouth, and looked, challengingly, at me.

The reason for my uncle's attachment to these animals lay not just in their extreme rarity but in his having known personally their discoverer and namesake—Hoffmeier himself.

This German-born zoologist had worked and studied at Frankfurt until forced to leave his country for London during the nineteen-thirties. The war years had suspended an intended programme of expeditions to the Congo and the Cameroons, but in 1948 Hoffmeier had gone to Africa and come back with the remarkable news of a hitherto unidentified species of pygmy antelope. In the interval he had made his permanent home in London and had become friends with my uncle, who started at the Zoo more or less at the time of Hoffmeier's arrival in England. It was by no means a common thing, then, for a serious and gifted zoologist to befriend a zealous but unscholarly animal keeper.

Hoffmeier made three more trips in the next ten years to Africa and carried out intensive studies of the "Hoffmeier" and other species of forest antelope. Then in 1960, fearing that the already scant Hoffmeier's Antelope, prized for its meat and pelt by local hunters, would be no more within a few years, he had brought back three pairs for captivity in Europe.

This was the period in which blacks and Europeans killed each other mercilessly in the Congo. Hoffmeier's efforts to save not only his own skin but those of his six precious charges were a zoological feat with few parallels. Two of the pairs went to London, one to Frankfurt, Hoffmeier's old zoo before the rise of the Nazis. The animals proved extremely delicate in captivity, but a second, though, alas, smaller generation was successfully bred. The story of this achievement (in which my uncle played his part), of how a constant and anxious communication was kept up between the mammal departments at Frankfurt and London, was no less remarkable than that of Hoffmeier's original exploits in the Congo.

But the antelopes stood little real chance of survival. Four years after Uncle Walter showed us his little trio there remained, out of a captive population that had once numbered ten, only three—the female we had seen as a scarcely credible baby, and a pair in Frankfurt. Then, one winter, the Frankfurt female died; and its male companion, not a strong animal itself, which had never known the dark jungle of its parents, was rushed, in hermetic conditions, accompanied by veterinary experts, by jet to London.

So Uncle Walter became the guardian of the last known pair of Hoffmeier's Antelopes, and therefore, despite his lowly status, a figure of some importance and the true heir, in the personal if not the academic sense, of Hoffmeier.

"Hoffmeier," my uncle would say at those Sunday afternoon teas, "Hoffmeier... my friend Hoffmeier..." His wife would raise her eyes and attempt hastily to change the subject. And I would seem to see the chink in his none too well fitting armour.

I was to live with him for some four months (it would be more accurate perhaps to say, "those last four months") when I first came to London after taking my degree. This was only a short while after my Aunt Mary's death following a sudden illness. I had got a job at the North London Polytechnic, and while I found my feet and looked for a flat it was agreed between Uncle Walter and my family that his home in Finchley, now half empty, should also be my own.

I accepted this kindness with misgivings. Uncle Walter welcomed me with morose hospitality. The house, with its little traces of femininity amongst the books and pipe-stands, was imbued with the sense of a presence which could not be replaced. We never spoke about my aunt. I missed her rock cakes and lemon-meringue. My uncle, whose only culinary knowledge had been acquired in preparing the diet of hoofed animals, ate large quantities of raw and semi-cooked vegetables. At night, across the passage-way that separated our rooms, I would hear him belch and snore vibrantly in the large double bed he had once shared, and, waking myself later in the night, would listen to him mutter solemnly in his sleep—or perhaps not in his sleep, for he wore now the shrouded look of a man wrapped in constant internal dialogue with himself.

Once, finding the bathroom light on at three in the morning, I heard him weeping inside.

Uncle Walter left before I woke to start his day at the Zoo; alternatively he worked late shifts in the evening—so that days passed in which we scarcely met. When we did he would speak coldly and shortly as if attempting to disguise that he had been surprised in some guilty undertaking. But there were times when we coincided more happily; when he would fill his pipe and, forgetting to light it, talk in that pedantic, pontifical, always "dedicated" way, glad to have me to debate with. And there were times when I was glad—since Uncle Walter had procurred for me a free pass to the Zoo—to slip from the traffic, the blurred faces of a city still strange to me, into the stranger still, but more comfortingly strange community by the banks of the Regent's Canal. He would meet me in his keeper's overalls, and I would be led, a privileged visitor, required to wear special rubber boots, into the breeding units closed to the public, to be shown—snuffling disconsolately at their concrete pen—the pair of frail, timid, wan-faced Hoffmeier's Antelopes.

"But what does it mean," I once said to Uncle Walter, "to say that a species exists which no one has ever observed?" We were talking in his front room about the possibility of undiscovered species (as the Hoffmeier's Antelope had once been) and, conversely, of near-extinct species and the merits of conservation. "If a species exists, yet is unknown—isn't that the same as if it did not exist?"

He looked at me warily, a little obtusely. In his heart, I knew, there lurked the slender hope that somewhere in the African forest there lived still a Hoffmeier's Antelope.

"And therefore," I continued, "if a thing which was known to exist ceases to exist, then doesn't it occupy the same status as something which exists but is not known to exist?"

My uncle furrowed his pasty brows and pushed forward his lower lip. Two nights a week, to make a little extra money, I was taking an evening class in Philosophy (for which I had no formal qualification) at an Adult Institute, and I enjoyed this teasing with realities. I would have led my uncle to a position where one might still assume the existence of an undiscoverable Dodo.

"Facts," he replied, knocking his pipe, "scientific data—sound investigatory work—like Hoffmeier's for example"—in a jerky shorthand which betrayed unease. I knew he was not a scientist at heart. Well read enough, privately, to pass for a professional zoologist, he would never have done so, for he liked, as he put it, to work "with" not "on" animals. But science, nonetheless, was the power he called, reluctantly, guiltily, to his aid whenever his ground was threatened.

"Science—only concerned with the known," he flung out with a pinched, self-constraining look; though a glint deep in his eye told me that he had already fully pursued and weighed my arguments, was open, despite himself, to their seduction.

"Whatever is found to exist or ceases to exist," I went on, "nothing is altered, since the sum of what exists is always the sum of what exists."

"Quite!" said my uncle as if this were a refutation. He settled back in his chair and raised to his lips the glass of frothy stout that stood on the arm-rest (Guinness was my uncle's one indulgence).

I wished to manoeuvre him towards the vexed question of why it was that—if we were prepared to admit the possibility of species that might never be discovered, that might live, die and vanish altogether, unrecorded, in remote forests and tundra—we should yet feel the obligation to preserve from oblivion, merely because they were known, creatures whose survival was threatened—to the extent, even, of removing them from their natural habitat, transporting them in planes, enclosing them, like the Hoffmeier's Antelopes, in antiseptic pens.

But I stalled at this. It seemed too sharp an assault upon a tender spot. Besides, I really felt the opposite of my own question. The notion that creatures of which we had no knowledge might inhabit the world was thrilling to me, not meaningless, like the existence, in maths, of "imaginary" numbers. Uncle Walter eyed me, moving his pipe from side to side between his teeth. I thought of the word "ruminant" which in zoology means "cud-chewer." I said, instead of what I had intended: "The point is not what exists or doesn't, but that, even given the variety of known species, we like to dream up others. Think of the animals in myth—griffins, dragons, unicorns..."

"Ha!" said my uncle, with a sudden piercing of my inmost thoughts which jolted me, "You are jealous of my antelope."

But I answered, with a perception which equally surprised me: "And you are jealous of Hoffmeier."

The plight of the two antelopes at this time was giving cause for anxiety. The pair had not mated when first brought together, and now, in a second breeding season, showed little further sign of doing so. Since the male was a comparatively weak specimen there was fear that the last chances of saving the animal from extinction, at least for another generation, were empty ones. Uncle Walter's role during this period, like that of other zoo officials, was to coax the two animals into union. I wondered how this was contrived. The antelopes when I saw them looked like two lonely, companionless souls, impossibly lost to each other even though they shared a species in common.

Yet my uncle was clearly wrapped in the task of producing an offspring from the creatures. Throughout those weeks after my aunt's death his face wore a fixed, haunted, vigilant look, and it would have been hard to say whether this was grief for his wife or concern for his issueless antelopes. It struck me for the first time—this was something I had never really considered, despite all those Sunday teas as a boy—that he and my aunt were childless. The thought of my uncle—lanky and slobbery, fingers and teeth stained indelibly amber, exhaling fumes of stout and raw onion—as a begetter of progeny was not an easy one. And yet this man, who could reel off for you, if you asked, the names of every known species of *Cervinae*, of *Hippotraginae*, teemed, in another sense, with life. When he returned home late on those March evenings, a dejected expression on his face, and I would ask him, with scarcely a trace, now, of sarcasm in my voice, "No?" and he would reply, removing his wet coat, shaking his bowed head, "No," I began to suspect—I do not know why—that he had really loved my aunt. Though he hardly knew how to show affection, though he had forsaken her, like a husband who goes fishing at weekends, for his animals, yet there was somewhere, unknown to me, in that house in Finchley a whole world of posthumous love for his wife.

My own love-life, in any case, occupied me enough at this time. Alone in an unfamiliar city, I acquired one or two short-lived and desultory girlfriends whom I sometimes took back to Uncle Walter's. Not knowing what his reaction might be, fearing that some spirit of scholarly celibacy lurked in the zoological tomes and in the collection of taxidermies, I took care to ensure these visits took place while he was out, and to remove all traces, from my front bedroom, of what they entailed. But he knew, I soon sensed, what I was up to. Perhaps he could sniff such things out, like the animals he tended. And my exploits prompted him, moreover, to a rare and candid admission. For one night, after several bottles of stout, my uncle—who would not have flinched from examining closely the sexual parts of a gnu or okapi—

confessed with quivering lips that in thirty years of marriage he could never approach "without qualms" what he called his wife's "secret regions."

But this was later, after things had worsened.

"Jealous of Hoffmeier?" said my uncle. "Why should I be jealous of Hoffmeier?" His lips twitched. Behind his head was an anti-macassar, with crochet borders, made by my aunt.

"Because he discovered a new species."

Even as I spoke I considered that the discovery might be only half the enviable factor. Hoffmeier had also won for himself a kind of immortality. The man might perish, but—so long at least as a certain animal survived—his name would, truly, live.

"But—Hoffmeier—zoologist. Me? Just a dung-scraper." Uncle Walter reverted to his self-effacing staccato.

"Tell me about Hoffmeier."

Hoffmeier's name, Hoffmeier's deeds sounded endlessly on my uncle's lip, but of the man himself one scarcely knew anything.

"Hoffmeier? Oh, expert in his field. Undisputed..."

"No—what was he like?" (I said "was" though I had no certain knowledge that Hoffmeier was dead.)

"Like—?" My uncle, who was preparing himself, pipe raised to stress the items, for the catalogue of Hoffmeier's credentials, looked up, his wet lips momentarily open. Then, clamping the pipe abruptly between his teeth and clutching the bowl with his hand, he stiffened into almost a parody of "the comrade recalled."

"The man you mean? Splendid fellow. Boundless energy, tremendous dedication. Couldn't have met a kinder... Great friend to me..."

I began to doubt the reality of Hoffmeier. His actual life seemed as tenuous and elusive as that of the antelope he had rescued from anonymity. I could not picture this stalwart scientist. He had the name of a Jewish impresario. I imagined my uncle going to him and being offered the antelope like some unique form of variety act.

I asked myself: Did Hoffmeier exist?

My uncle, poking his head forward oddly, in one of those gestures which made me think he could see my thoughts, said: "Why, he used to come here, stay here. Many a time. Sat in that armchair you're sitting in now, ate at that table, slept—"

But then he broke off suddenly and began to suck hard at his pipe.

I was having no luck in my attempts to find a suitable flat. London grew more faceless, more implacable, the more I grew accustomed to it. It did not seem a place in which to be a teacher of maths. My philosophy lectures became more esoteric. I gave a particularly successful class on Pythagoras, who, besides being a mathematician, believed one should abstain from meat and that human souls entered the bodies of animals.

Four weeks after my talk with Uncle Walter about Hoffmeier, things took a sudden bad turn. The male antelope developed a sort of pneumonia and the fate of the pair and—so far as we may know—of a whole species, seemed sealed. My uncle came in late from the Zoo, face drawn, silent. Within a fortnight the sick animal had died. The remaining female, which I saw on perhaps three subsequent occasions, looked up, sheepishly, apprehensively, from its solitary pen as if it knew it was now unique.

Uncle Walter turned his devotion to the remaining antelope with all the fervour of a widowed mother transferring her love to an only child. His eyes now had a lonely, stigmatized look. Once, on one of my Sunday visits to the Zoo (for these were often the only occasions on which I could be sure of seeing him), the senior keeper in his section, a burly, amiable man called Henshaw, drew me to one side and suggested that I persuade Uncle Walter to take a holiday. It appeared that my uncle had requested that a bed be made up for him in the antelope's pen, so that he need not leave it. A bundle of hay or straw would do, he had said.

Henshaw looked worried. I said I would see what I could do.

But, for all that I saw of my uncle, I scarcely had an opportunity to act on my promise. He came home after midnight, leaving a reek of stout in the hall, and sneaked straight upstairs. I felt he was avoiding me. Even on his off-duty days he would keep to his room. Sometimes I heard him muttering and moving within; otherwise an imprisoned silence reigned, so that I wondered should I, for his own sake, peer through the keyhole or leave behind the door a tray of his favourite fibrous food. But there were times when we met, as though by accident, in the kitchen, amongst his books in the front room. I said to him (for I thought only an aggressive humour might puncture his introspection) didn't he think his affair with the female antelope was going too far? He turned on me the most wounded and mortified look, his mouth twisting and salivating; then he said in a persecuted, embattled tone: "You been speaking to Henshaw?"

He seemed conspired against from all sides. One of the things that distressed him at this time was a proposal by the Council to build a new inner link road which, though it would not touch his own house, would cleave a path through much of the adjacent area. Uncle Walter had received circulars about this and subscribed to a local action group. He called the council planners "arse-holes." This surprised me. I always imagined him as living in some remote, antiquated world in which the Zoological Society, august, venerable, was the only arbiter and shrine. So long as he could travel to the warm scent of fur and dung, it did not seem to me that he noticed the traffic thundering on the North Circular, the jets whining into Heathrow, the high-rises and flyovers—or that he cared particularly where he lived. But one Saturday morning when, by rare chance, we shared breakfast and when the noise of mechanical diggers could be heard through the kitchen window, this was disproved.

My uncle looked up from his bowl of porridge and bran and studied me shrewdly. "Don't like it here, do you? Want to go back to Norfolk?" he said. His eyes were keen. Perhaps my disillusion with London—or maybe the strain of sharing a house with him—showed in my face. I murmured non-commitally. Outside some heavy piece of machinery had started up so that the cups on the table visibly shook. My uncle turned to the window. "Bastards!" he said, then turned back. He ate with his sleeves rolled up, and his bare forearms, heavily veined and covered with gingery hairs, actually looked strong, capable. "Bastards," he said. "Know how long I've lived here? Forty years. Grew up here. Your Aunt and I—. Now they want to..."

His voice swelled, grew lyrical, defiant. And I saw in this man whom I had begun to regard as half insane, a grotesque victim of his own eccentricities, a glimpse of the real life, irretrievably lost, as if the door to a cell had momentarily opened.

I began to wonder who my true uncle was. A creature who was not my uncle inhabited the house. When not at the Zoo he retired ever more secretively to his room. He had begun to remove to his bedroom from his "library" in the corner of the front room certain of his zoological volumes. He also took, from on top of the bookcase, the framed photographs of his wife. At three, at four in the morning, I would hear him reading aloud, as if from the Psalms or the works of Milton, passages from Lane's *Rare Species*, Ericdorf's *The African Ungulates* and from the work which I had already come to regard as Uncle Walter's Bible, Ernst Hoffmeier's *The Dwarf and Forest Antelopes*. In between these readings there were sporadic tirades against certain absent opponents, who included the borough planning committee and "that shit-can" Henshaw.

The fact was that he had developed a paranoiac complex that the world was maliciously bent on destroying the Hoffmeier's Antelope. He was under the illusion—so I learnt later from Henshaw—that, like children who believe that mere "loving" brings babies into the world, he could, solely by the intense affection he bore the female antelope, ensure the continuation of its kind. He began to shun me as if I too were a member of the universal conspiracy. We would pass on the stairs like strangers. Perhaps I should have acted to banish this mania, but something told me that far from being his enemy I was his last true guardian. I remembered his words: "The speed of the cheetah, the strength of the bear..." Henshaw phoned to suggest discreetly that my uncle needed treatment. I asked Henshaw whether he really liked animals.

One night I dreamt about Hoffmeier. He had a cigar, a bow tie and a pair of opera-glasses and was marching through a jungle, lush and fantastic, like the jungles in pictures by Douanier Rousseau. In a cage carried behind him by two bearers was the pathetic figure of my uncle. Watching furtively from the undergrowth was a four-legged creature with the face of my aunt.

The attendances at my philosophy classes fell off. I devoted two lessons to Montaigne's "Apology of Raymond Sebond." Students complained I was leading them along eccentric and subversive paths. I did not mind. I had already decided to quit London in the summer.

My uncle suddenly became communicable again. I heard him singing one morning in the kitchen. A thin, reedy, but strangely youthful tenor was crooning "Our Love is Here to Stay." He had changed to the afternoon shift of duty and was preparing himself an early lunch before heading for the Zoo. There was a smell of frying onions. When I entered he greeted me in the way he used to when I was a Sunday guest, just grown into long trousers. "Ah Derek! Derek, me lad—have a Guinness," he said, as though there were something to celebrate. He offered me a bottle and the opener. There were already four empties on the draining board. I wondered whether this was a miraculous recovery or the sort of final spree people are apt to throw before flinging themselves off balconies. "Uncle?" I said. But his sticky lips had parted in an inscrutable grin; his face was contained and distinct as if it might disappear; his eyes were luminous, as though, should I have looked close, I might have seen in them the reflections of scenes, vistas known only to him.

I had with me a file of students' work in preparation for my afternoon's maths classes. He looked scoffingly at it. "All this—" he said. "You ought to have been a zoo-keeper."

He wiped his mouth. His long sallow face was creased. I realized that nowhere could there be anyone like my uncle. I smiled at him.

That night I had a telephone call from Henshaw. It must have been about one in the morning. In a panic-stricken voice he asked me if I had seen Uncle Walter. I said no; I had been teaching at the adult institute, finished the evening at a pub and come home to bed. My uncle was probably already in bed when I came in. Henshaw explained that a security officer at the Zoo had found various doors to the special care unit unlocked; that on further investigation he had discovered the pen of the Hoffmeier's Antelope empty. An immediate search of the Zoo precincts had begun but no trace was to be found of the missing animal.

"Get your uncle!" screamed Henshaw maniacally. "Find him!"

I told him to hang on. I stood in the hallway in bare feet and pyjamas. For one moment the urgency of the occasion was lost in the vision I had of the tiny creature, crossing the Prince Albert Road, trotting up the Finchley Road, its cloven feet on the paving stones, its soft eyes under the street-lamps, casting on North London a forlorn glimmer of its forest ancestry. Without its peer in the world.

I went up to Uncle Walter's room. I knocked on his door (which he would often keep locked), then opened it. There were the books scattered on the floor, the fetid remnants of raw vegetables, the shredded photos of his wife . . . But Uncle Walter—I had known this already—was gone.

GABOR

"THIS IS GABOR," SAID MY father in a solemn, rehearsed, slightly wavering voice.

This was early in 1957. The war was still then quite fresh in the memory—even of those, like myself, who were born after it. Most households seemed to have framed photographs of figures in uniform, younger Dads, jauntily posed astride gun barrels, sitting on wings. Across the asphalt playground of my County Primary School the tireless struggle between English and Germans was regularly enacted. This was the only war, and its mythology ousted other, lesser intrusions into peace. I was too young to be aware of Korea. Then there was Suez, and Hungary.

"Gabor, this is Mrs. Everett," continued my father, enunciating slowly, "Roger's Mummy. And this is Roger."

Gabor was a lanky, dark-haired boy. He was dressed in a worn black jacket, a navy blue jumper, grey shorts, long grey socks and black shoes. Only the jacket and limp haversack, which he held in one hand, looked as if they were his. He had a thick, pale, straight-sided face, dark, horizontal eyes and a heavy mouth. Above his upper lip—I found this remarkable because he was only my age—was a crescent of gossamer, blackish hairs, like a faint moustache.

"Hello," said my mother. Poised in the doorway, a fixed smile on her face, she was not at all clear what was to be done on occasions like this—whether motherly hugs or formality were required. She had half expected to be ready with blankets and soup.

Father and the newcomer stood pathetically immobile on the doorstep.

"Hello Gabor," I said. One adult custom which seemed to me, for once, eminently practical, and vindicated by moments like this, was to shake hands. I reached out and took the visitor's wrist. Gabor went a salmony colour under his pale skin and spoke, for the first time, something incomprehensible. Mother and Father beamed benignly.

Gabor was a refugee from Budapest.

He was largely Father's doing. As I see it now, he was the sort of ideal foster-child he had always wanted; the answer to his forlorn, lugubrious, strangely martyrish prayers. Father had been an infantry officer during the war. He had been in North Africa and Normandy and at the liberation of concentration camps. He had seen almost all his friends killed around him. These experiences had given him the sense that suffering was the reality of life and that he had, in its presence, a peculiarly privileged understanding and power to reassure. Peace was for him a brittle veneer. He was not happy with his steady job in marine insurance, with the welfare state blandishments of those post-ration years. The contentments of fatherhood were equivocal. Now, as I look back, I see him waiting, watching over me, the corners of his stern mouth melancholically down-turned, waiting for me to encounter pain, grief, to discover that the world was not the sunny playground I thought it to be; so that he could bestow on me at last—with love I am sure—the benefits of his own experience, of his sorrow and strength, the large, tobaccoey palms of his protection.

I must have hurt him. While he lived with his war-time ghosts, I was Richard Todd as Guy Gibson, with an RT mask made from my cupped hand, skimming ecstatically over our back lawn to bomb the Möhne Dam; or Kenneth More as Douglas Bader, cheerily cannonading the Luftwaffe.

Father scanned the newspapers. At headlines of trouble and disaster he looked wise. When the news broke of the uprising in Hungary and its suppression, and later the stories of orphaned Hungarian children of my generation coming to our shores, who needed to be found homes, he acquired a new mission in life.

I did not take kindly to Gabor's arrival. Though he was not a proper adoption and was to be with us at first only on what the authorities called a "trial basis," I was envious of him as as substitute child—a replacement for myself. A minor war, of a kind unenvisaged, between England and Hungary, might have ensued in our house. But I saw how—from the very start—I had a facility with Gabor which my parents did not, and the pride I derived from this checked my resentment. Besides, Gabor had the appeal of someone who—like my father—had lived through real bloodshed and conflict, though in his case the experience was of the present, not of the past, and belonged moreover to a boy my own age. Perhaps—unlike my father—he would share in, and enhance, the flavour of my war games.

Should this happen it would assuage another long-standing grievance against my father. I could not understand why, seasoned veteran as he was, he did not participate in, at least smile on, my imaginary battles. I began to regard him as a bad sport and—more serious—to doubt his own quite authentic credentials. I tried to see in my father the features of my cinema heroes but failed to do so. He lacked their sunburned cragginess or devil-may-care nonchalance. His own face was pasty, almost clerical. Consequently I suspected that his real exploits in the war (which I had only heard about vaguely) were lies.

The first lesson in English manners I taught Gabor was how to shoot Germans.

When I reflect on this, it was remarkable that he grasped what was required of him. Not only did he scarcely know a word of English, but there was an historical difficulty. I had absolutely no knowledge of Hungary's role in the Second World War (I was ignorant of its collaboration with the Nazis), which I took to be a national duel between England and Germany. Nonetheless, when the smoke from our bren guns or hand grenades had cleared, and I informed Gabor, after bravely reconnoitering, of another knocked out Panzer, another slaughtered infantry patrol, he would look up at me with implicit trust and grin, manically, jubilantly.

"*Jó*," he would say. "Good, good."

Father was horrified at the careless zeal with which Gabor took part in my games. He could not understand how a boy who had known real violence, whose own parents (for all we knew) had been brutally killed, could lend a part so blithely to these fantasies. Some impenetrable barrier—like a glass wall which gave to my father the forlorn qualities of a goldfish—existed for him between reality and illusion so that he could not cross from one to the other. But it was not just this that distressed him. He saw how Gabor looked to me and not to him, how when he returned from our forays at the end of the garden Gabor would follow me like a trusted commander; how, from the very beginning, that affinity which he had hoped to have with this child of suffering had eluded him. I often wondered how they had managed together on that first day, when father had gone up to "collect" Gabor, like some new purchase. I pictured them coming home, sitting mutely on opposite seats in the train compartment as they bounced through suburbia, like two lost souls.

"Gabor," Father would say as he lit his cigarette after dinner, with the air of being about to make some vital announcement or to ask some searching question.

"*Igen?*" Gabor would say. "Yes?"

Father would open his lips and look into Gabor's face, but something, some obstacle greater than that of language, would leave his words trapped.

"Nothing."

"Yes?"

Gabor would go pink; his eyes would swivel in my direction.

Later, when Gabor had acquired a little more English, I asked him whether he liked my father. He gave a rambling, inarticulate answer, but I understood it to mean from the manner in which it was spoken that he was afraid of him. "Tell me about your own mother and father," I asked. Gabor's chin trembled, his lips twisted, his eyes went oily. For two days not even the prospect of Messerschmitts to be shot down persuaded him to smile.

Gabor went to my primary school with me. Except when he had special language tuition he was scarcely ever out of my company. He was an intelligent boy and after eighteen months his English was remarkably fluent. He had a way of sitting in the class with a sad expression on his face which made all the teachers fall for him. I alone knew he was not really sad. My closeness to Gabor gave me a superior standing among my English friends. Gabor would now and then mutter phrases in Hungarian because he knew this gave him a certain charisma; I would acquire even more charisma by casually translating them. In our newly-built brick school, with its grass verges and laburnums, its pictures of the Queen, maps of the Commonwealth and catkins in jam-jars, there was very little to disturb our lives. Only the eleven-plus hung, like a precipice, at the end of it all.

In the summer holidays Gabor and I would play till dark. At the end of our garden were the ramshackle plots of some old small holdings, and beyond that open fields and hedges sloping down to a road. These provided limitless scope for the waging of all types of warfare. We would scale the fence at the end of the garden, steal venturously past the tumbled sheds and smashed cucumber frames of the small holdings (still technically private property) and into the long grass beyond (later they built a housing estate over all this). At one point there was a sizeable crater in the ground, made by an actual flying-bomb in the war, filled with old paint cans and discarded prams. We would crouch in it and pretend we were being blown up; after each grisly death our bodies would be miraculously reconstituted. And everywhere, amongst the brambles and ground-ivy, there were little oddities, and discoveries, holes, tree-stumps, rusted tools, shattered porcelain, debris of former existences (I believed it was this ground-eye view of things which adults lacked), which gave to our patch of territory infinite imaginary depths.

A few impressions are sufficient to recapture that time: my mother's thin wail, as if she herself were lost, coming to us from the garden fence as the dark gathered: "Roger! Gabor!"; Gabor's hoarse breath as we stalked, watching for enemy snipers, through the undergrowth, and the sporadic accompaniment, as if we shared a code, of his Hungarian: "*Menjünk! Megvárj!*"; Father, trying to restrain his anger, his disappointment, as we trailed in finally through our back door. He would scan disapprovingly our sweaty frames. He would furrow his brows at me as if I was Gabor's corruptor, and avoid Gabor's eyes. He would not dare raise his voice or lay a finger on me because of Gabor's presence. But even if Gabor had not been there he would have been afraid to use violence against me.

Father would not believe that Gabor was happy.

In the summer in which I waited with foreboding to hear the result of my eleven-plus, and Gabor also waited for his own fate to be sealed (he had not sat the exam, the education committee deciding he was a "special case"), something happened to distract us from our usual bellicose games. We had taken to ranging far into the field and to the slopes leading down to the road, from which, camouflaged by bushes or the tall grass, we would machine-gun passing cars. The July weather was fine. One day we saw the motor-bike—an old BSA model (its enemy insignia visible through imaginary field-glasses)—lying near the road by a clump of hawthorn. Then there was the man and the girl, coming up one of the chalk gulleys to where the slope flattened off—talking, disappearing and reappearing, as they drew level with us, behind the banks and troughs of grass, like swimmers behind waves. They dipped for some time behind one of the grass billows, then appeared again, returning. The man held the girl's hand so she would not slip down the gulley. The girl drew her pleated skirt between her legs before mounting the pillion.

The motor-cycle appeared the next day at the same time, about five in the hot afternoon. Without saying anything to each other, we returned to the same vantage point the following day, and our attention turned from bombarding cars to stalking the man and the girl. On the fourth day we hid ourselves in a bed of ferns along the way the couple usually took, from which we could just see, through the fronds, a section of road, the top of the gulley and, in the other direction, at eye level, the waving ears of grass. Amongst the grass there were pink spears of willow herb. We heard the motor-bike, heard its engine cut, and saw the couple appear at the top of the gulley. The girl had a cotton skirt and a red blouse. The man wore a T-shirt with sweat at the arm-pits. They passed within a few feet of our look-out then settled some yards away in the grass. For a good while we saw just the tops of their heads or were aware of their presence only by the signs of movement in the taller stems of grass. Sounds of an indistinct and sometimes hectic kind reached us through the buzzing of bees and flies, the flutter of the breeze.

"*Mi az?*" whispered Gabor. "*Mit csinálnak?*" Something had made him forget his English.

After a silence we saw the girl sit up, her back towards us. Her shoulders were bare. She said something and laughed. She tilted her head back, shaking her dark hair, raising her face to the sun. Then, abruptly turning round and quite unwittingly smiling straight at us as if we had called her, she presented to us two white, sunlit, pink-flowered globes.

On the way back I suddenly realised that Gabor was trying not to cry. Bravely and wordlessly he was fighting back tears.

It so happened that that day was my parents' wedding anniversary. Every July this occasion was observed with punctilious sentimentality. Father would buy, on his way home from work, a bottle of my mother's favourite sweet white wine. My mother would cook "Steak au Poivre" or "Duck à l'Orange" and put on her organdie summer frock with bits of tulle around the neckline. They would eat. After the meal my father would wash up, sportingly wearing my mother's frilled apron. If the evening was fine they would sit outside, as if on some colonial patio. My father would fetch the Martell. My mother would put on the gramophone so that its sound wafted through the open window, "Love is a Many Splendoured Thing" by Nat King Cole.

In previous years, given an early supper and packed off to bed, I had viewed this ritual from a distance, but now, perhaps for Gabor's sake, we were allowed to partake. Solemnly we sipped our half-glasses of sweet wine; solemnly we watched my parents. Inside, we still crouched, eyes wide, amongst the ferns.

"Fifteen years ago," Father explained to Gabor, "Roger's mother and I were married. Wed-ding ann-i-versary," he articulated slowly so that Gabor might learn the expression.

I looked at Gabor. He kept his head lowered towards the tablecloth. His eyes were dry but I could see that at any moment they might start to gush.

Mother and Father ate their steaks. Their cutlery snipped and scraped meticulously. "Gorgeous," my father said after the second mouthful, "beautiful." My mother blinked and drew back her lips obligingly. I noticed that, despite her puffy dress, her chest was quite flat.

Gabor caught my eyes. Some sorrow, some memory of which

none of us knew, could no longer be contained. Father intercepted the glance and turned with sudden heed towards Gabor. For the first time that evening something like animation awoke in his eyes. I could imagine him, in a moment or so, pushing aside the remainder of his steak, rejecting with a knitting of his brows the bottle of Barsac, the bowl of roses in the middle of the table, grasping Gabor's hand and saying: "Yes, of course, this is all nonsense..."

But this was not to be. I was determined, if only to defy father, that Gabor would not cry. There was something in our experience of that afternoon, I recognised, for which tears were only one response. Gabor relowered his head, but I pinned my gaze, like a mind-reader, on his black mop of hair, and now and then his eyes flashed up at me. A nervous, expectant silence hung over the dinner table, in which my parents resumed eating, their elbows and jaws moving as if on wires. I saw them suddenly as Gabor must have seen them—as though they were not my parents at all. Each time Gabor looked up I caught his eyes, willing them not to moisten, to read my thoughts, to follow my own glance as I looked, now at my father's slack jowl, now at Mother's thin throat.

Gabor sat in front of the window. With the evening light behind him and his head bent forward, his infant moustache showed distinctly.

Then suddenly, like boys in church who cannot restrain a joke, he and I began to laugh.

I learnt that I was to be accepted at a new grammar school. Gabor, by some inept piece of administration, was granted a place at a similar, but not the same institution, and arrangements were made for continuing his private tuition. The whole question of Gabor's future, whether or not he was to be formally adopted into our family, was at this stage "under review." We had till September to pretend we were free. We watched for the couple on their motor-bike. They did not reappear. Somehow the final defeat or destruction of the last remnants of the German army, accomplished that summer, did not compensate for this. But our future advance in status brought with it new liberties. Father, whose face had become more dour (I sometimes wondered if he would be glad or sorry if the authorities decided that he could legally be Gabor's father), suggested that I might spend a day or two of our holiday showing Gabor round London. I knew this was a sacrifice. We had gone to London before, as a family, to show Gabor the sights. Gabor had trailed sheepishly after my parents, showing a token, dutiful interest. I knew that Father had had a dream once, which he had abandoned now, of taking Gabor by himself up to London, of showing him buildings and monuments, of extending to him his grown man's knowledge of the world, his shrewdness in its ways, of seeing his eyes kindle and warm as to a new-found father.

I took Gabor up on the train to London Bridge. I knew my way about from the times Father had taken me, and was a confident guide. We had fun. We rode on the Underground and on the top decks of buses. In the City and around St. Paul's there were bomb-sites with willow-herb sprouting in the rubble. We bought ice-creams at the Tower and took each other's photo in Trafalgar Square. We watched Life Guards riding like toys down the Mall. When we got home (not long before Father himself came in from work) Father asked, seeing our contented faces: "Well, and how was the big city?" Gabor replied, with the grave, wise expression he always had when concentrating on his English: "I like London. Iss full history. Iss full history."

THE HYPOCHONDRIAC

I REMEMBER THAT DAY FOR two things. It was a bright, keen day in mid-September. Autumn had come. Everything was sharp and conspicuous...

Firstly, it was that day that my wife and I learnt that she was pregnant. She gave me the sample in the morning. I took it myself to be tested at the hospital. Perhaps it is strange for a doctor to be clinical even with his own wife. I handed the sample to McKinley in the lab and said, "I'll wait for this one—it's my wife." A little while later McKinley returned: "Positive." But even before this my wife had known—those early intuitions are often right—that she was really pregnant. We ought to have been glad. When I'd left that morning with the sample I looked at her lingeringly—to see, perhaps, if her intuitions went any further. The sun was dazzling in our kitchen. She turned away, and then I kissed her, lightly, on the top of the head, as one kisses an unhappy child. When McKinley said, "Congratulations," it took an effort to make the usual display of pleasure...

And then it was that day that I first saw M. He was the last on my list for evening surgery, and I knew somehow, as soon as he entered, that he was a fake. He spoke of headaches and vague pains in the back and chest. He was a slight, bland, dull-looking youth of barely twenty. You can tell when someone is describing a pain that isn't really there.

"What sort of pain?"

"A kind of stabbing."

"Are you getting it now?"

"Oh yes—it's always there."

"A constant *stabbing* pain?"

I sounded his chest, took his pulse and went through a few other motions just to please him. At length I said to him: "I'd say you're a perfectly fit young man. You're physically sound. Are you worried about anything? I think this pain of yours is quite imaginary. I think you've imagined it enough to make it actually exist. But that doesn't mean it's anything." I said this kindly enough. I really wanted to say: "Oh go away." I wanted to have finished surgery and be alone. I ushered him to the door. He had this pale, ineffectual face which I disliked. At the door he suddenly turned and said: "Doctor, the pain's quite real"—with such earnestness that I said hastily (this was a mistake), "If you're still worried come and see me next week."

Then he was gone down the gravel path leading from my waiting room.

I hadn't seen my wife since the morning. I'd phoned her from the hospital. I said, "It's positive—congratulations," just to see if she would react as I had done to McKinley. She said, "Well I knew." Then I had matters to attend to at the hospital, a meeting with the radiologist, some calls in the afternoon; and when I returned I got straight on with my evening surgery without even going into the house. This is not unusual. My surgery and waiting room are an annexe of the house, but my wife and I look upon them as distinct zones. My wife never enters my surgery even out of surgery hours; and there are times—that evening was one—when I feel more at home at my surgery desk than in the house which is only the other side of a door.

I said good-night to Susan, my receptionist, and pretended to be busy with some record cards. It was not quite seven. The sun which had shone all day was low, but bright, crisp and ruddy. Through my surgery window I could see the apples swelling on the apple trees in our back garden, the orange berries on the pyracantha, the virginia creeper turning red on the house wall. I have always been pleased by the way the garden is visible from my surgery and presses in on it as if on some sort of conservatory. I think my patients find this reassuring. Often they remark gladly on the view. I sat for some time at my desk looking at the garden. I didn't want to think of my wife. I thought of my Great-Uncle Laurie. Then I looked at my watch, got up and locked the outer doors of the waiting room and surgery, and passed through the connecting door into the house. As I did so I put on a cheerful, earnest face, as I do for my patients. My wife was in the kitchen. She is twenty-nine, young enough to be my daughter. I took her in my arms but with scarcely any pressure, the way one touches something fragile and precious. She said: "Well, we will have to wait and see."

M. came to my surgery the week following his first visit, and the week after that, and at intervals right through that winter. I was wrong in ever wavering on his first visit. I summed him up as a hypochondriac of the thorough-going kind. For one thing there was his persistence. For another, there was the seemingly infinite adaptability of his symptoms and the discrepancies in his description of them. For example, when, on one visit, I had dismissed some localized pain as purely fictional, he would return a second time to tell me that the pain had "travelled"—from chest to lower abdomen, from heart to kidneys—so that I was obliged to reconsider it. After a while this "pain" became something omnipresent and amorphous, obscurely pervading his system but ready to fix itself in those regions where he imagined, I suppose, I would be least able to disregard it. He would often describe in some detail the classic symptoms of certain complaints—the sort of thing anyone can read in medical encyclopaedias—but he would forget some tell-tale associative factor or he would fail to reproduce the physical signs. Then he would fall back on his old stand-by: "But Doctor, the pain's quite real," and I on mine: "For God's sake—there's nothing wrong with you."

I could not be rid of him by merely rebutting his complaints. It occurred to me, of course, that there was another line to be taken. M.'s hypochondria itself, palpably neurotic, was the only thing about him which could be legitimately treated clinically. I should have questioned him about his mental history, his anxieties, perhaps referred him for psychiatric treatment. But I did not do this. It seemed to me that to take M.'s condition seriously would quite probably have the effect of indulging and encouraging it rather than removing it. I could not suppress the suspicion that he was carrying out some elaborate joke at the expense of medicine and I did not want to fall victim to it. Besides, I had no wish to extend an already excessive interest, on his part, in disease. There is nothing I despise more. Don't mistake me. I did not become a doctor out of an interest in disease, but because I believe in health. The fact that half my family were medical men makes no difference to my motives. There are two ways of confronting disease: one is sound practical knowledge; the other is health. These are the two things I value most. And health, believe me, is not the absence of but the disregard for disease. I have no time for the mystique of suffering.

So I could give M. nothing more than the crude advice that a thousand would-be patients give themselves—very effectively: "Forget about it. It's nothing. You're fine." And I said: "I don't want to see you here again."

But he did come again, and he was an infernal nuisance. There were times when I had to restrain myself from shouting at him at the top of my voice, from grasping hold of him and ejecting him bodily from my surgery. Sometimes a quite violent hatred for that despondent face, for his pleading manner rose inside me. I wanted to hit him. Then I would begin to treat him with a kind of casual indifference—the way a bartender treats a regular customer who comes in every night and drinks alone at the bar, cheerlessly but harmlessly. Then I would get angry again; angry at M., angry at my own acquiescence. "Look," I said, "I have really ill people to attend to. Do you know what really ill people are? You are wasting my time and preventing me from helping people who really require help. Go away. *Do* something! Take up ski-ing or mountaineering—then perhaps you might find yourself in genuine need of a doctor!" But he would not be beaten: "I *am* really ill."

Once when I had shown him out I noticed that my hands were shaking; I was quite distraught.

"Who *is* that man?" my wife said.

We were sitting, about to have lunch, in our dining room, which looks out across the front garden onto the road. On the opposite side of the road is a bus-stop where sometimes, after I have finished surgeries, my last visitors can still be seen waiting for their buses. My wife sees my patients come and go. She asks about them. Sometimes I think she is jealous of them.

M. was there, in his crumpled blue raincoat. My wife must have noticed him before.

"That's M." I said. "He's a damn nuisance." And then I added in a sudden defensive, possesive way—I don't know why: "There's nothing wrong with him! Nothing wrong with him at all!"—so that my wife looked back at me in a startled fashion.

This was a short while before Christmas. My wife's pregnancy was now quite visible. I have helped countless women through their pregnancies. This has given me satisfaction. But this baby, inside my wife, was like a barrier between us.

I said to M. about a week later (we were back to headaches and miscellaneous complaints, the jumbled up symptoms of half a dozen nervous disorders): "You know just as well as I do that you're perfectly fine, don't you? Why do you do it?"

It was a raw, foggy day in November. On such a day my surgery can seem cosy, a place of sanctuary. I have a fine oak desk with a roll top, a dark green carpet, a gas fire that fizzes gently; pictures on the wall—still-lifes of flowers and fruit.

I had put my pen down on my desk and leant back in my chair. I was ready to talk frankly.

"I am not well, Doctor—I come to you."

There was sometimes something foreign about M.'s voice, his accent, his choice of phrase, his looks.

I sighed and swivelled slowly in my revolving chair.

"Tell me about yourself. What do you do? You're some sort of clerk aren't you?"

"Life insurance."

This amused me. I didn't show it.

"But what about your evenings? Weekends?"

He said nothing. He looked uneasily at my desk. He was like a schoolboy who clams up when the master becomes friendly.

"Don't you have friends? A girlfriend?"

No answer.

"Family?"

He shook his head.

His expression was empty and opaque. Without pressing him further I could see the whole picture: filing and entering figures all day; a bed-sit somewhere, evenings spent alone. At night he would lie awake listening to his heart-beat, the suction of his lungs, the gurgling of his alimentary canal.

I thought of myself when I was twenty. I had pored over

textbooks in the Medical School library. I had played Rugby for Guy's; dated a girl from the Dental School.

"Well—" I began.

"Doctor," he interrupted as if impatient with my digression. He had this way, despite his reticence, of suddenly pulling you up. "You are going to tell me what's wrong?"

"Well, I was about to say that if you lead a fuller—"

"No, I mean what's wrong with *me*." He patted his chest. Sometimes he spoke as if I were withholding from him some awful truth. "Please tell me."

"The same as usual—nothing," I said crossly.

"You know that?"

"Yes."

"How can you know?"

This was like a game of bluff in some interrogation.

"It's my job, for goodness sake."

He drew his face a little closer to mine. It had the same sheepish look it perpetually wore, but there was something insistent, arresting about it.

"Doctor, you have to relieve pain. Do you know what pain is?"

I should have blown up at an absurd comment like this, gently spoken though it was. But I didn't. I noticed I was swivelling quite compulsively from side to side in my chair. I had taken up the fountain pen from the desk and was rolling it between my fingers.

"Look, all this is rather pointless, don't you think? We don't seem to be any help to each other. Shall we call an end to the game now? Don't you think it's gone far enough?"

He blinked.

"Come on, off with you."

He got up. I was stern. But, in speaking to him in that confiding way, I realized that I had admitted that he had got under my skin, that he affected me, that my relations with him were different—more intimate and involved—from my relations with other patients. At the door he looked up, almost with satisfaction. My palms sweated. His features had this flat quality, as if there was nothing behind them. And suddenly I knew why he fostered and cherished his "pains," why he manufactured little upheavals and crises in his body, why he needed these amateur dramatics in my surgery: He was getting his experience.

That night my wife could not sleep. She had a mild pregnancy ailment for which I had had tablets prescribed. We lay awake in the dark. I said to her (this was a question I had been asking her, silently, ever since we knew she was pregnant, but now I spoke it aloud): "Whose child is it?" "How do I know?" she said. And yet I knew she knew. Perhaps she was not saying, to protect me, to propitiate me; or—if it was my child—to punish me. She turned onto her side. I put my hand gently on her belly.

I met my wife when she was twenty-two and I was forty-one and had just become a partner in the practice which I run now by myself. I had trained and worked for twenty years in the hectic world of hospitals and acquired something of a reputation; but it was never my aim to become eminent in medicine, to devote myself exclusively or academically. One day I wanted to take up a practice which I could manage without hardship, where I would be free to enjoy life. I would enjoy life. I had a taste, a zest for it. My medical knowledge would ensure this—you see, it was always for me a matter of health, of happiness. And when I took up this practice it would be time for me to marry. My wife would be young, sensual, free, full of life. She would make up for some of the sacrifices, for some of the constraints that go with serving medicine.

Barbara was these things. Though she had also, I imagined, an appearance of being vulnerable, of needing to be protected, of being in some ways, despite her twenty-two years, still a child.

She worked in the Haematology Unit at St. Leonard's. I have always had a special interest in haematology. This is because once I was frightened by blood. I used to be scared of the sight of it. Barbara had been at St. Leonard's for a year, after graduating. Within eighteen months we married. Perhaps I wooed her in an old-fashioned manner. By showing her the solid things I had to offer: the house with its adjoining surgery which Dr. Bailey (a man who had studied under my great-uncle at Bart's) would offer me when he retired and I took on his practice; the garden with its apple trees; my professional standing; my knowledge. Perhaps it was she who looked to me for a widening of experience. She was playful, energetic, capricious and I wanted to share these things as an equal. But I found myself falling into the role of the older man whose dignity is being teased, tempted. We went on our honeymoon to Italy. We made love in a room with bleached shutters overlooking the Gulf of Sorrento. And yet after this I knew it was not to be as I had foreseen. I did not let this trouble me; I have learnt not to let things trouble me, to accept what is so. I regarded my wife's youth as perfectly natural, perfectly right, even if I could not wholly reciprocate it. I began to look on her as a father looks on a daughter: Her pleasure was my pleasure; I was there to advise her, to safeguard her pleasure, to protect it from what risks it might incur, to ensure her health. I did not want to restrain her. We started to divide off the surgery and the house as separate territories so as not to impose on each other. Perhaps she became jealous of my patients because the attention I gave them was in a way similar to that I gave her. Yet I believe I was considerate to her, as I was to my patients. I would think of all I had; I had every reason to be thankful. I would look at my wife, as she prepared herself, her hair up, for an evening with friends or as she stepped, laden with carrier bags, from the car I bought her (only sometimes would I tell myself, these visions are like photographs whose real subject you do not touch—but I did not let this trouble me), and I would think: I am a happy man, a really happy man. And then I began to want a child.

I knew she was having an affair with Crawford. He was the new head of the Haematology Unit. Only thirty-two. I was not angry, or recriminatory. I don't believe in making suffering. I thought: This is natural and excusable; she must have this adventure; she must have her experience. The best treatment is to let it run its course. When it is over she will come back to me and our relations will be stronger, more cheerful. I was not even jealous of Crawford. He was a non-medic, like most of the staff in research departments. He had all the non-medic's sense of a subject seen in academic isolation away from its human bearing. He was a rather slight, unprepossessing man—if sixteen years my younger. His affair with Barbara lasted through that summer, and ended in August. I do not know if he broke it off or whether they put an end to things mutually because they felt guilty at what they were doing to me. Or to Crawford's wife. Later I learnt that Crawford was accepting a job in Canada in the new year. Barbara took the break-up badly; she even cried in front of me and blamed me. I thought: This is to be expected, it will heal; life begins again. They had terminated the affair just before she and I went on our summer holiday, in the west of Ireland. Often I would leave her in our room and I would go for strolls along the beach or over the golf links, breathing the clean air with gratitude.

Then, when we returned, we learnt that she was pregnant.

I put my hand gingerly on her belly. When you feel the belly of a pregnant woman you can tell all sorts of things about the child she carries. Except whose it is.

"Tell me," I said.

"I don't know, I don't know."

I thought: All this is perhaps a pretence, to create drama.

"If you tell me, I will understand. Either way."

She did not answer. It was as though she was far away. She

was hunched up beneath the bedclothes, gathered into herself, like the foetus inside her.

After a long pause she said: "What will you understand?"

A few days later, when M. appeared in my surgery, I turned upon him furiously. I refused to treat him. I had not meant to behave like this. But at the sight of his helpless face something exploded inside me. It was no longer a case of professional annoyance. I felt I must be free of him as one feels sometimes one must break off a harmful relationship, sever a tie one should never have begun. "Out!" I said, "I've had enough! Out!" He looked at me with a kind of ingenuous disbelief. This made me all the more severe. "Out! I don't want to see you again!" I could feel my face was flushed and I was losing control. "But—my pain is *real*, Doctor," he reiterated his old cry. "No, your pain is not real," I said emphatically. "If it were real, you would not be concerned whether it were real or not." This made me feel more in command. One of my hands was on M.'s shoulder pressing him towards the door. I opened it and all but pushed him out. "Go, will you? I don't want to see you again!"

It was a dark evening in mid-winter. A light over my surgery door lit up the gravel path. He walked away, but paused momentarily, after three or four steps, to look back at me over his shoulder. And as he did so I suddenly had a strange, intense memory from when I was a boy. I was no more than eleven. It was one warm summer Sunday when all the family was in the garden. I had gone indoors into the kitchen for some reason and found our old tom cat Gus dead on the floor. It was lying on the tiles with its legs straight out beside it. I knew it was dead, but I had never encountered death in such a tangible form before. I was frightened. But what frightened me was not so much the dead cat itself but the fact that I was the first to discover it, so that in some way its death was tied up with me, I had responsibilities towards it. I did not know what to do. I simply retreated into the garden, pretending to have seen nothing and trying to hide my state of mind, till someone else made the discovery. But, as I crept out of the kitchen door and down the side path, I had looked back, involuntarily, as if in some way the dead cat might rise up to expose my guilt and cowardice, like the ghost of a murdered corpse.

This memory flashed through my mind as M. departed, but not in the usual way of such memories, as if you see everything again, through your own eyes. I seemed to be looking at myself, from the outside, as a young boy, just as in reality I was now looking at M.

I returned to my desk and sat down. "What on earth was all that about?" said my receptionist, coming in from the little office adjoining my surgery. The shouting must have penetrated almost to the waiting room. "It's all right Susan. It's okay. Give me a moment or so, would you, before you send the next one in." She went out again. I sat at my desk for several minutes with my head in my hands. My surgery is built projecting back from the side of the house so that the rear windows of the house are visible, obliquely, from it. Similarly, by looking from the house one can see the windows of the surgery. I drew back the blinds above my desk and looked at the lit ground floor windows where I knew Barbara would be. I wanted her to appear. Then I drew a breath and pressed the buzzer on my desk which was a signal to call the next patient from the waiting room.

When surgery was over that evening I locked up at once and went straight through to my wife. I wanted to put my arms around her and hold her protectively. But somehow she forestalled me. "What's the matter?" she said. She was standing in the hallway drying her hands with a kitchen towel. Perhaps I still looked agitated from my outburst with M. She came towards me. She guided me through to the living room. "Here, you sit down for a while, you don't look so good." I was so surprised by this that I let myself be led. During the early years of our marriage when it became clear that the difference in our ages would have its effect, my wife had sought a new interpretation of her role. She had seen herself, at some time in the future, as the younger, stronger partner, keeping a watchful, soothing eye over a busy, older husband, guarding him against the strains of over-work. I had resolved that she would never have the opportunity to do this. She motioned me towards a chair. I thought: This is ridiculous, it is some kind of trick. I am the doctor: She is saying I look unwell. It is I who was about to comfort her; it is she who needs rest. As she pressed me to sit down I suddenly thrust her hands off me. "I'm okay, for God's sake." She looked at me piercingly. "All right then," she said, and her expression went grim and hollow.

Later that evening it struck me why it seemed I sometimes recognized M.'s face. His face was like the face of one of the corpses we had dissected in anatomy classes when I was a student. I remembered it because nearly all the corpses used by medical schools are of old people. I did not suffer myself from the attacks of squeamishness which afflict most medical students in the dissecting room. But this corpse, of a young, slim-built man, made me pause. The anatomy lecturer had joked about it. "Your age, eh Collins?"

It's the same face, I thought. But I dismissed the notion from my mind.

Two or three days after that I received a telephone call which made my heart sink. It was from a young woman who said she was speaking on behalf of M. She said she had a room in the house in which M. lived. M. was ill. He had attracted the attention of other people in the building and given them my number. I thought: Of course, the inevitable ploy. Now he is forbidden my surgery. It was impossible to explain my position over the telephone, impossible, too, to say outright that I had no intention of visiting M. I said that I would try to fit in a call later that afternoon. It was then about eleven in the morning. In my anger I did not even go through the usual practice of asking for a description of symptoms.

"He seems bad, Doctor, don't you think you should come at once?"

I was tempted to say, "It's all an act, you stupid girl, don't let him fool you," but I didn't. Her voice seemed genuinely imploring. I said, briskly, instead: "Look, I'm a busy man, I can't come before four—all right?" And slammed the receiver down.

I had in fact several calls to make that day. Some were of a quite serious nature, none were, strictly, urgent. I knew I had a duty to deal with an emergency first. Some emergency! My only difficulty lay in deciding whether I should go to M.'s at all. I did not make up my mind until I had finished my other calls. Usually I like to complete my rounds by four so that I can have a moment's peace before evening surgery at five. It was nearly a quarter past four when I turned the car round and headed in the direction of M.'s. I knew there could be unpleasant consquences for a doctor who refuses a call, even a false alarm, where third parties are concerned. I arrived at M.'s address—one of a row of large, ugly Victorian houses with basements—at about half-past. It was almost dark. More than one person seemed to be waiting for me as the door was opened: a girl with frizzed hair and glasses whom I took to be the telephone caller, a tall, laconic West Indian, a middle-aged man in a blue cardigan who appeared from a room at the rear, another woman, on the stairs, leaning over the banisters. I knew at once they were hostile. The woman on the stairs, who was furthest from view, spoke first:

"You're too bloody late mate!"

The girl in glasses explained: "We called an ambulance."

"You did what?"

"It left half an hour ago—we were really worried."

"Well what was wrong for God's sake?"

"*Now* he asks," said the West Indian, looking me up and down. "Five hours," he added, "five fuckin' hours for the doctor to come."

I stood in the hallway in my overcoat, holding my doctor's bag. I couldn't help thinking that all this—even the ambulance—was still some pretence, a hoax, an elaborate conspiracy to continue M.'s fraud. I didn't want to commit the error of finding it real. The hallway was dimly lit and unheated.

Scraps of tattered lino covered the floor and stairs. Smells of cooking mingled in the air. The people in front of me were like characters in some stage thriller in which I took the role of prime suspect. Everything was strange.

I managed to hold on to myself sufficiently to say: "Look, M.'s been coming to see me for some time—I'm quite aware of his condition. Now"—I turned to the girl in glasses—"I gather it was this young lady who phoned me this morning. I'd like to talk to her—alone. I'd be grateful if you others allowed me to do so."

They looked at me for a while as if they had no intention of moving, then, slowly, they slunk away. The West Indian said over his shoulder to the girl: "You tell him, Janie!"

We went to the girl's room on the first floor. It was a gloomy, cluttered room, relieved by coloured rugs over the chairs and potted plants on the mantel-piece. She lit a cigarette and spoke readily but with suspicion in her voice. She described a collection of varied, incoherent symptoms—like the ones M. described to me in my surgery—which added up to nothing precise in my mind. I listened impassively. When she saw that I appeared unimpressed it became plain that she disliked me. I thought: If I could tell her.

"Any vomiting, fever—flushes, rashes?" I asked.

She shrugged as if it were my business to observe such things. "Doctor, he was crying out in pain—he was in agony."

"I see."

I said that I would like to see M.'s room. I don't know why this was important to me. She said hesitantly, "All right. It's the one next door. I took the key when the ambulance left."

As we moved along the passageway I asked, "Do you know him? Has he been here long?"

"Keeps to himself. Quiet. We thought he was foreign at first. We'd like to see him more but we don't push."

"Lonely?"

"Perhaps."

The woman who had spoken first when I arrived appeared again on the stairs. "Poor boy, never no trouble to anyone."

"Yes," I said.

M.'s room was a complete contrast to what I had seen of the rest of the house. Everything smacked of neatness, cleanliness, order. The bed, along the wall, was dishevelled, but apart from this the furniture—an armchair, a coffee table, a table with two wooden chairs, a chest of drawers and a wardrobe—seemed fixed in prescribed positions and unused, as if in a room unoccupied and waiting for guests. There were no clothes or newspapers left lying about, no odds and ends on the mantel-piece. In one corner, in an alcove, there was a sink and draining board, a work-surface with two gas rings and a kettle, and cupboards above and below. All this was old, chipped and corroded, but there were no dirty plates left in the sink, no uncleared food, and the draining board was wiped clean. There was nothing in the room to indicate the life that used it—save perhaps the books, in a double row of shelves, over the bed: a small, varied collection thinly covering a wide range of topics, like the books of a schoolboy who has many subjects to learn. Amongst them I noticed, with sour satisfaction, the faded spine of an old Black's Medical Dictionary. All this depressed me and made me uneasy. I looked around M.'s bed and opened a small bedside cupboard. I don't know what I hoped to find—a cache of empty chemist's bottles, the disordered notes of some amateur self-diagnosis. There was nothing. "He's not 'on' anything, if that's what you think," said the girl, now quite open in her reproaches. We moved towards the door. Before we went out into the passage I took a last look round and I knew what made me feel uneasy, even threatened. It was the room of an innocent, a child, waiting for life to upset it.

Before I left I said to the girl: "Thank you. I'll get in touch with the hospital. I am sorry I wasn't here earlier but, if you'll believe me, I don't think there's any real cause for alarm."

She nodded coldly.

I drove back. I felt calm, as far as M. was concerned. But I had this forboding inside, as though for myself. I got back late to open surgery. I did not phone St. Leonard's until six. I knew who should be the senior duty doctor in Casualty.

"Tony? It's Alan Collins here. Have you got a patient of mine there? Name's M."

"Yes—we have"—the voice seemed to modify itself rapidly—"I'm afraid we have. He's dead."

"Dead?"

For several seconds I was unable to say anything else. I wanted to know why Tony should trick me.

"About an hour ago. Nearly a DOA case. You're his GP?"

"But what the hell from, for Christ's sake?"

"Well—we were rather hoping you might be able to tell us that."

I did not tell my wife about M.'s death. For ten days or so I had to assimilate the fact of it myself, to face the autopsy reports and inquest (which could reach no certain conclusions about the causes of M.'s death, other than the immediate ones of sudden coma and respiratory failure) and the possibility of an inquiry, which was waived, into my own professional conduct. Throughout all this I had to overcome a feeling that something had cracked inside me, that some firm footing on which I had previously relied had given under me. I suppose I was suffering from shock and mental stress of a quite clinical order. I said to myself: Look at this as you would the case of some patient of yours. I became incommunicative and withdrawn. I stayed in my surgery long after evening surgery had finished. Susan noticed the change in me, so did my surgery patients, and so, of course, did Barbara. If I had told her everything and sought her comfort I dare say it would have helped. But I had already refused her attention once when she'd said I looked ill; and, besides, it was I who had said so heatedly to her, weeks ago, that there was nothing wrong with M. In any case I had become—how shall I put this?—suddenly afraid of my wife, of the fact of her pregnancy. I don't know why. It was as if her fullness matched a void I felt in myself.

She must have seen all this only as coldness and indifference. It was February. She was nearly seven months pregnant. One night, as she lay in bed, she began to sob—long, heavy, breathless sobs, as if she had been quite abandoned. When I put my arm round her she moaned: "It's his child, it's his child. I know it." Then for a long while she said nothing but only continued sobbing, the sobs growing louder into helpless groans, her face in her hands, her body shuddering. I tried not to hear the sobs. I said to myself: In a crisis you must try to ignore the pain, the cries. I sat by my wife in my pyjamas, holding her sides as if to repress her sobs. I did not know if I believed her. I said at length: "I understand." And then, after another interval: "I wish it had been my child." She raised herself up and turned to me—her tears made her look like something alien, like a monster: "It would have been worse if it was your child." And she held her face, taut, in front of mine until I looked away.

In the surgery the next morning I avoided the eyes of my patients. I wrote out prescriptions rapidly and tore them off the pad. Perhaps they saw that something was wrong. I wanted surgery to be over; but it was the dead, worn-out end of winter—endless "chests," coughs and rheumatic pains. After perhaps fifteen visitors had left I pressed my buzzer yet again. I had got up to return something to my filing cabinet. When the door was opened my head was lowered. I said, "One moment," then turned towards the person who had entered. I said, "What?" and stepped forward. And it must have been then that I collapsed, for I remember nothing else, save being helped off the floor and into my chair, my patients in the waiting room being sent away, Susan bending over me, and, later, Barbara.

It was M. I had seen.

Now I sit in the armchair in the living room by the rear window, the telephone and my pills on the table beside me. If I look along the wall of the house I can just see him, through a chink in the blinds in the surgery: Mason, my substitute, bending over the desk, getting up and moving out of sight to examine a patient, like some ghost of myself. He has been my "temporary" replacement now for nearly ten weeks. They say I cannot work again yet. Long and complete rest is indicated. I don't know—if it were my case—if I would prescribe this. First it was my colleagues who looked after me. I saw their grudging faces—no doctor likes to treat another doctor, it's a sort of ill omen. Then it was Barbara. Though she needed tending herself, it was she who cared for me. And I had no choice but to submit. Perhaps there was a change here; perhaps she became happier, these last ten weeks. I don't know. For a while I was like the child she mothered.

It is a bright, fresh morning towards the end of April, breezy—warm and chill at the same time. In the garden I can see daffodils and the white sprays of blossom on the apple trees, whipped by sudden gusts. Somewhere in the maternity wing at St. Leonard's my wife is about to give birth to a baby. If I were not under contrary orders I would be there. Perhaps she is being delivered at this very moment. I wait, by the telephone, catching glimpses of Mason and watching the wind play in the garden.

It was under the apple trees that Great-Uncle Laurie used to sit on warm summer days in the big garden we had when I was small, constantly filling his mouth with titbits, swilling expensive wine and smoking his endless fat cigars.

I admired him then; though I had feared him once. He was a surgeon at Bart's; a senior surgeon of renown, who had performed his first operations in the days of chloroform and ether, when the standard surgical dress was waistcoat, apron and rolled sleeves. There were photographs of Uncle Laurie with bits he had removed from patients. I feared him, as I feared all my mother's family—uncles, great-uncles—with their black coats and eyes that seemed to look into your insides; but I feared Great-Uncle Laurie most, with his saws and bone-chisels.

I did not understand, you see, how you could live without fear. I was ignorant and naive,

But, more than this, I did not understand how Uncle Laurie, who had opened people up for a living, could retire (when I was nine), put away his instruments and devote himself thereafter to food and drink; how a man whose business had been with disease could ignore his own knowledge and the strictures of his doctor and grow fat, short-winded, red-faced and sedentary. Under the apple tree he looked perfectly at peace with the world. And this made me fear him more. He saw my fear. "What are you afraid of?" he said. And to my mother: "That boy will grow up a bundle of nerves unless you do something about it."

But it was he who did something—that afternoon our cat died.

My mother had gone into the kitchen, discovered the body, thinking she was the first to do so, and returned at once to inform us all. Everyone wondered how to dispose of the corpse. I hung my head, but Uncle Laurie watched me. While the others fussed he said: "Come with me. *We'll* dispose of him—leave the boy with me awhile." And he got up slowly from his wicker chair, stubbing his cigar out irritably.

He led me into the garage and squeezed his bulk with difficulty alongside our car, to the work bench at the rear. He cleared some tools off the bench, placed a piece of oilcloth over the space and then a wooden board over the cloth. His arms were massive, but at the end of them were precise, agile fingers like a pianist's. He fixed the car inspection-lamp, with its long flex, on the work bench in such a way that its light fell on the board, combined with the light from the rear garage window. "Now," he said, "before the thing's too stiff." He waddled out of the garage and returned after a while bearing Gus in one arm and in the other a black leather bag containing scalpels, forceps and probes.

"You're afraid of these things eh? Of dead animals? Watch."

And then, in what seemed a mere handful of minutes, Uncle Laurie pinned the cat to the board, opened it up, pointed out to me its vital organs, demonstrated how it had lived, performed its functions and died—of a heart attack—briefly related the physiology of cats to that of human beings and gathered together the remains for burial.

He talked in a detached monotone, his face heavy and disinterested, as if his mind was on something else.

Throughout all this I was not allowed to turn my eyes from the foraging of the scalpel. My head was pushed forward so I would see better and miss nothing. I breathed Gus's internal odours.

"You see, there is nothing to worry about when you know what is there and you know how it works."

He gave a sort of satisfied grunt. Perhaps he was proud of his performance; though I did not see him smile. He wiped his instruments clean with a kind of ponderous disdain, as if, if he wished, he could put Gus's parts together again, like a motor, and bring him back to life.

Later I saw him in the garden sucking a peach.

But I knew now why he could sit so contentedly under the trees, enjoying his cigar and the sunshine on his face, why he could make himself fat and breathless, careless of the consequences. You see, health is not the absence of but the disregard for disease.

That day I knew I would become a doctor.

I watch Mason moving behind the chink in the blinds in the surgery. I don't know if I believe in ghosts. As a doctor, a man of science, it is not my business to believe in such things. When a doctor is sick there are all kinds of suspicions, all kinds of proverbial stigmas. Perhaps my patients will leave me like some Victorian country doctor implicated in a scandal. Outside in the garden the daffodils are bending and little snow-storms of blossom are being shaken from the apple trees. My wife is having a baby. I think of this as something terrible, as if she is about to be torn in two. I should not have such preposterous thoughts. I sit in my slippers and cardigan by the window, propped up by cushions, waiting for the telephone.

I don't know if it was M. I really saw in my surgery. I don't know if my wife really knows if it is Crawford's child. I know very little.

Uncle Laurie died when I was fourteen, of obesity and fatty degeneration. When we buried him I mourned for him no more—this was a mark of my admiration—than I did for Gus when we buried him in the rockery. I had thought he was happy, healthy, at peace. He needed no one's grief. Only now do I see that he was slowly killing himself. All he had been was a brilliant surgeon, a first-rate physician; expert in his field. He was gorging himself to fill up the gaps. He was filling himself up because his life was empty.

THE TUNNEL

ALL THAT SPRING AND SUMMER Clancy and I lived on the third floor of the old grey-brick tenement block in what might have been—we never really knew—Deptford or Bermondsey, Rotherhithe or New Cross. It was cheap because the block was due for demolition in the autumn and all the tenants had notice to quit by September. Most of them had gone already, so that those who remained were like survivors camping in a ruin. The vacated rooms were broken into at night and became the sources of foul smells. The old cream paintwork of the stair-wells, which here and there had darkened like enormous nicotine stains, was daubed with aerosol slogans and obscenities, and all through that hot drought of a summer the dust and litter from the streets, old pages of newspapers and polythene bags found their way up the flights of stairs, even as far as the third floor.

We didn't mind. It was all we could afford. We even relished the way we scooped out for ourselves a little haven, oblivious of the squalor around us. We were very young; we had only just left school. We were absorbed with each other, and we didn't think about what we'd do in a month's time, or two months', or when the winter came or we had to find somewhere else to live. We made love insatiably, the way very young people in love can. And when that summer arrived, endlessly sunny and hot, we thought of it as a blessing on ourselves, despite the dust and the smells, because it was possible to live quite well in that room, with its scant furniture, draughty windows and twin gas ring, so long as the weather was good. We even saved on the few clothes we had between us, because, most of the time, with the dirty windows up and the hot air swimming in from the street, we wore nothing at all.

We had run away because that was the only way Clancy and I could go on seeing each other without Clancy's parents stopping us. We hadn't run far. Clancy's parents lived in a big, elegant Regency house by the park in Greenwich, and we knew that by going a couple of miles away, into the kind of area they preferred to think didn't exist, we'd be as safe as if we'd fled to the ends of the country. Clancy's father was a sort of financial expert who acted in an advisory capacity to the government and knew people in the House of Lords, and her mother came from good, sound pedigreed stock. They were not the kind of people to drag the police into a hunt for their daughter. But it was not beyond them to employ some private agency to track us down. And this was one of the reasons why, despite the scorching weather, we seldom left our third floor room, and when we did we kept a sharp eye open for men in slow-moving cars hugging the kerb, who might suddenly pull up, leap out and bundle Clancy inside.

Clancy's family was small. There were only Clancy herself, her mother and father and an ageing uncle who lived in seclusion in an old manor house in Suffolk where Clancy had spent summers when she was small. Clancy's father was obsessively proud of the fact that he was descended from a once noble line which could be traced back to the reign of Henry VIII; and—like Henry VIII himself—he had turned cold, as Clancy grew up, towards his wife and daughter because they were a perpetual reminder that he had no son. There was nothing, apparently, he could do to change this fact; but he was dead-set on preventing the only remaining eligible member of the family from being absorbed into the riff-raff.

I only met Clancy's mother and father once, and that was by accident one Saturday afternoon when Clancy had promised me her parents wouldn't be back till late. I had gone to the house in Greenwich. We made love on Clancy's bed, looked at her photo albums and listened to the Beach Boys. We were sitting under the vine in the conservatory and Clancy was urging me to sample her Dad's stock of malt whisky, when her parents suddenly turned up, having changed their plans for the evening. Clancy's father asked me in icy, eloquent tones who the hell I thought I was and told me to get out. It was as if my presence in the house had no connection whatsoever with Clancy, as if I were some random, alien intruder. He was a tall, poised, steel-haired man with an air of having had the way of dealing with such situations bred into him and of merely summoning it automatically when required. I remember thinking that he and Clancy's mother, and perhaps Clancy too, belonged to some completely foreign world, a world that had ceased to exist long ago or perhaps had only ever existed in people's minds; so that whenever I thought of Clancy's parents, looking out from our tenement window, I had to make an effort to believe they were real.

My own parents were no obstacle to us. They had had me late in life, so there was a big gap between our ages, which, oddly enough, smoothed our relations. They did not care what I did with my life. They had a council house in Woolwich and no shining example to set me. I'd gone to a large comprehensive; Clancy had gone to a classy girls' school in Blackheath; and we might never have known each other if it wasn't for Eddy, a big, hulking, raw-faced boy, who later joined the Royal Artillery, who told me in his matter-of-fact way that he had robbed two girls from Clancy's school of their virginity; and urged me to do the same. With rather less swagger, I followed Eddy's bidding ("Tell them they'll thank you for it afterwards"), but, unlike Eddy, I found the initial conquest wasn't an end in itself.

Clancy's parents soon found out—Clancy had a knack of defiant truthfulness. I don't know what outraged them more: the knowledge that their daughter was no longer intact and the possible scandal of some schoolgirl pregnancy—or the mere fact that Clancy associated with a boy from a council estate. I knew what I would say to Clancy's father if I ever had to face him. I would repeat to him something I'd read in the letters of Gauguin (my favourite artist at that time and the only artist I knew anything about). Gauguin says somewhere that the Tahitians believed, unlike Europeans, that young people fall in love with each other because they have made love, not the other way round. I would explain that Clancy and I were good, regular Tahitians. But when the opportunity arose that Saturday afternoon—despite the sun shining through the vine leaves in the conservatory and Clancy's thin summer dress and the malt whisky in my head—Gauguin's South Sea paradise, which was only an image for what I felt for Clancy, paled before the cold aplomb of her father.

But Clancy's uncle did not share the parental disdain. This I discovered in about our third week in the tenement. Clancy had to go out now and then to draw money from her Post Office account, which was our sole source of income at that time. One day she returned with, of all things, a letter from her uncle. Apparently, she had written to him, explaining everything, confident of his trust, immediately after our flight, but for complete security had not given an address and had asked him to reply via a Post Office in New Cross. Clancy showed me the letter. It was written in a shaky hand and was full of fond platitudes and breezy assurances, with a certain wry relish about them, to the effect that Clancy had enough sense now to lead her own life.

I said: "If he's so much on our side, why don't we go to him?" And I had a momentary vision, in Bermondsey, of dappled Constable landscapes.

"That's just where they'll look for us first."

"But he won't tell them that you've got in touch."

"No."

And then Clancy explained about her uncle.

He had always had a soft spot for her and she for him, since the days when she used to play muddy, rebellious games round his estate in the summer. As she grew up (her uncle lost his wife and his health declined), it became clear that there were strong temperamental differences between him and her parents. He did not care for her father's sense of dignity or for his precious concern for the family name. He would be quite happy, he said, to sink heirless beneath the Suffolk soil. And he disapproved of the way Clancy was being rigorously groomed for some sort of outmoded high society.

"So you see," said Clancy, putting away the letter, "I had to tell him, didn't I? It's just what he'd want."

She kissed the folded notepaper.

"And another thing"—she got up, pausing deliberately before she went on. "I know for a fact when Uncle dies I'll get everything; he won't leave a thing to Mum and Dad. So you see—we're all right."

She said this with a kind of triumph. I realised it was an announcement she must have been saving up till the right moment, in order to make me glad. But I wasn't glad—though I put on a pleased expression. I'd never really reflected that this was what Clancy's background meant—the possibility of rich legacies, and I had never seen myself as a story-book adventurer who, having committed a daring elopement, would also gain a fortune. Nevertheless, it wasn't these things which disturbed me and (for the first time) cast a brief shadow over my life with Clancy. It was something else, something I couldn't understand. Clancy stood, smiling and pleased, at the window with the sun coming in behind her. She was wearing jeans and one of those tops made from gauzy, flimsy materials which she liked, I think, precisely because when she stood in front of the light you could see through them. It was the first fine weather of the spring, the first time we had been able to lift up our window wide to let some of the stinking air from inside out and some of the less stinking air from outside in. We'd been living together for three weeks, fugitives in a slum. The way happiness comes, I thought, is as important as the happiness itself.

From our tenement window you could see all that was ugly about that part of London. Directly opposite, across the road, was a junior school—high arched neo-Gothic windows, blackened brickwork, a pot-holed asphalt playground surrounded by a wall with wire netting on top—which, like the tenement, was due to be pulled down at the end of the summer. It stood at the edge of an area, to the left as we looked from the window, which had already been demolished or was in the process of being demolished. Everywhere there were contractors' hoardings, heaps of ruined masonry and grey corrugated metal fencing. Old blocks of terraced houses got turned into brick-coloured wildernesses over which dogs prowled and paths got trodden where people took short cuts. To the right, on the other side of the school, there was an odd, inexplicable path of worn grass with a stunted tree and a bench on it, and beyond that, on the other side of a side street with a few tattered shops, was another wasteland—of scrap yards, builders' yards, half defunct factories and fenced-off sites which seemed to be depositories for cumbersome, utterly useless articles: heaps of car axles from which the oil ran in black pools, stacks of rusted oil drums, even a pile of abandoned shop-window dummies, their arms and legs sticking up like some vision from Auschwitz. Beyond this was the railway line to London

Bridge on its brick arches, the tower blocks, precincts and flimsy estates which had sprouted from previous demolitions; while if you looked far round to the right you could see the nodding antennae of cranes by the Thames.

All this we could survey at leisure, but because we were on the third floor, when you lay on the bed (which we did most of the time) and looked out of the window, you saw only the sky. When the good weather came we lifted up the sash window high and moved the bed according to the position of the gradually shifting rectangle of sunshine, so that we could sunbathe most of the day without ever going out. We turned nice and brown and I told Clancy she was getting more and more like the cinnamon-coloured South Sea girls Gauguin painted.

We would lie looking up at the blue sky. Now and then we'd see flights of pigeons and gulls, or swallows swooping high up. All day long we could hear the noise from the street, the demolition sites and the breakers' yards, but after a while we got accustomed to it and scarcely noticed it. We could tell time was passing by the periods of commotion from the school playground. We joked about our bed being a desert island, and made up poems about ourselves and our room in the style of John Donne.

I began to wish that when we'd hastily packed and fled I'd brought more books with me. All I had was my life of Gauguin and *Sonnets, Lyrics and Madrigals of the English Renaissance* which I'd borrowed from my English master at school and never given back. I thought of my old English master, Mr. Boyle, a lot now. He had a passion for Elizabethan poetry which he vainly tried to transmit to members of the fourth and fifth year, who laughed at him, I amongst them, and spread rumours that he was queer. Then in my last year, after I'd met Clancy, I suddenly began to appreciate his poems, their airy lucidity and lack of consequence. I think Mr. Boyle thought all his efforts were at last rewarded. He pressed books on me and wrote fulsome comments on my work. And I longed to tell him it was all only because of Clancy, because she was light and lucid like the poems—because we'd lost our innocence together but kept it, because we'd made love one wet Thursday in a secluded part of Greenwich Park...

I read aloud from Mr. Boyle's book, lying naked in the sunshine on the bed. I wondered if he could have foreseen its being read like this. Clancy wriggled at bits she liked. A lot of the poets were obscure, little known men with names like George Turberville and Thomas Vaux. We tried to imagine what they had looked like and who the mistresses were they wrote to, and where they fucked them, in four-posters or in cornfields. Then Clancy said: "No, they were probably not like that at all. They were probably cold, scheming men who wanted positions at court and wrote poems because it was the done thing." She would say sudden sharp, shrewd things like this as if she couldn't help it. And I knew she was right.

"Like your Dad, you mean," I said.

"Yes." Clancy laughed. Then I told her how her Dad reminded me of Henry VIII, and Clancy said there was an old hollow tree in Greenwich Park where Henry VIII fucked Anne Boleyn.

At night, because of the heat and because we hardly moved during the day and only tired ourselves by making love, we would often lie awake till dawn. Clancy would tell me about her uncle's estate in Suffolk. There was a crumbly red-brick house with tall chimneys and a stable yard, a lawn, a walled orchard and a decaying garden with a wood at the end. Through the wood and across a stretch of heath was the tail of an estuary, winding up from the sea. Marshes, river walls and oyster beds; the smell of mud and salt. There was a tiny wooden jetty with two rowing boats moored to it which were beached high in the mud when the tide went out, and in hot weather, at low tide, the sun cooked the mud so that when the water returned it was warm and soupy for swimming. In the marshes there were shelduck and redshanks—once she had seen an otter—and in the wood there were owls which you could hear hooting at night from the house.

When I listened to Clancy describing things in such detail I would be amazed by the fact that she'd done all these things, years ago, and I'd never even known she existed. And I'd long for the impossible—to have gone down those same paths with her, watched the same marsh birds, swum in the same muddy water when she and I were little more than infants. As she rambled on we'd hear the trains clacking to and fro along the railway. Once, just as she was talking about the owls in the wood we heard a ship hooting on the Thames. And for most of the night there'd be a strange mixture of noises from the tenement itself: radios and TVs and people arguing, an old man's cough and the sound of bottles smashing, the noise the kids made invading the stairs and the yells and threats when somebody tried to drive them out. But we hardly let this bother us, and, even in that area of London, there came a time when, while Clancy babbled, you could imagine that outside there were mud-flats and marshes and meadows with dykes and sluice-gates; just as at other times, when we'd try to remember lines from *Romeo and Juliet* which we'd both done for "O" level, we'd try to imagine that instead of the scrap yards and junk tips there were the piazzas and bell-towers of Verona.

"What's your uncle like?" I asked Clancy.

"He's a randy old bastard who can't do anything about it because he's stuck in a wheel-chair." Clancy smiled. "You'd like him, he's like you."

I said I didn't have a wheel-chair.

"I didn't mean that."

"How old is he?"

"Seventy-three."

"What's he do?"

"In weather like this, he sits out in the orchard with this nurse in a bikini who brings him drinks. He used to paint a bit—watercolours—before his illness."

I was lying on my front and Clancy was stroking the backs of my legs. I couldn't imagine myself in a wheel-chair.

"How ill is he? Seriously?"

"Pretty ill. It's the winters. It gets cold there. The house isn't in such wonderful condition, you know." I realised that Clancy was speaking as if of some future home. "He nearly died last winter."

I pictured Clancy's uncle sitting out in the orchard with his voluptuous attendant, enjoying perhaps his last summer.

I said, "Do you think he's happy."

"I think he's happier now—since my aunt died—than he's ever been. But then he's an invalid."

When Clancy became exhausted with talking about Suffolk she would ask me about Gauguin. I said he was a French stock-broker who gave up his job to be a painter. He left his wife and family and went to Tahiti, where he lived with a native girl, painted his greatest pictures and died, in poverty, of syphilis.

One day Clancy was gone a long while on one of her trips to the Post Office. I was worried. I thought her parents' spies had swooped at last. But then she returned, sweating, with the money, a carrier-bag of shopping and a lumpy brown paper parcel. "Here," she said, kissing me and taking off her blouse, "For you." Inside the parcel there were six assorted pots of watercolour paint and a set of three brushes.

"You ought to be a painter," Clancy said. And after a moment's pause, "—or a poet."

"But you shouldn't have bought this. We need the money."

"It's my money."

"But—I don't know how to paint. I haven't painted since I was a kid."

"That doesn't matter. You've got the feel for it. I can see. You ought to be an artist."

I thought of explaining to Clancy that admiring an artist or two wasn't the same as possessing their gifts.

"But what am I going to paint on? I've got nothing to paint on."

Clancy quickly gulped down a mug of water from the sink and waved her hand. "There's all that—and all that." She pointed to two walls of the room from which the wallpaper had either been stripped back to the bare plaster or peeled of its own accord. "You can use the draining board as a palette. If you like, you can paint me." And she pulled off the rest of her clothes and bounced onto the bed, hair tossed back, one knee raised, one arm extended.

So I began to paint the walls of our room. I quickly forgot my initial doubts at Clancy's whim and made up for them with gratitude. I suppose I was really flattered and touched by the idea Clancy had of me, which only corresponded to some idea I secretly nursed of myself, as an artist, producing wonders in some garret.

My painting lacked skill, and the subjects were predictable—palm trees, paradisial fruits, lagoons, native girls in flowered sarongs, all stolen from Gauguin. But I knew what I was really painting and Clancy knew what I was really painting and what it meant. Each native girl was intended to be Clancy; and each one, it was true, was slightly less crude and ungainly than its predecessor, so that one day I really hoped to capture Clancy in paint. All through the early part of June I painted the first wall, while Clancy wrote to her uncle, describing my great talents and saying how few people truly understood life. To be happy and occupied seemed easy. You found a place of your own and made love. You rented a squalid room in Bermondsey and painted Polynesian scenes on the wall. Clancy's more extravagant fancies didn't seem to matter. Once she wrapped her arms round my neck as I cleaned my brush: "I had a letter from Uncle today. When we go to Suffolk you'll paint there, and write poems, won't you? All the painters painted there." I didn't answer this. As for being a poet, I didn't get beyond *Sonnets and Lyrics of the English Renaissance*. I was content as we were.

Then things changed. Nothing fundamental altered, but a host of minor things that had never bothered us before began to affect us. The dirt of our room and the smells of the tenement which we'd been heedless of up till then because we were preoccupied with each other, began to irritate us. This was odd because it was just at the time when I was transforming our little hole into a miniature Tahiti that we began to sense the filth around us. Before, we'd tipped all our rubbish, empty tin cans, milk cartons and vegetable peelings, into old grocery boxes till they overflowed, and we'd hardly noticed the stink or the swarms of flies. Now we bickered over whose turn it was to carry the rubbish boxes down to the dustbins at street level. We felt our lack of changes of clothes, even though we seldom wore any. Before, we used to wash clothes, because it was cheaper than the launderette, in an old two-handled zinc tub we'd found propped under the sink; and we'd washed ourselves in the same way, one of us sitting in, laughing, while the other tipped water over us. Now Clancy began to hanker after showers and proper laundering. Somehow we stopped thinking the same things together and wanting to do the same things at the same time—make love, eat, sleep, talk—which had meant that in the past there was never any need for decisions or concessions. Now the slightest things became subjects for debate. We began to get insecure about being found out and dragged back to the homes we'd left, even though we'd survived for nearly three months; and at night the noises in the tenement, the scufflings and shouts on the stairs made us nervous. Clancy would start up, clutching herself—"What's that?! What's that?!"—as if the police or some mad killer were about to burst in at the door.

Even the endless sunshine, which was such a blessing to us, began to feel stale and oppressive.

We were aware at least of one, unspoken reason for all this. Our money was dwindling. The figures in Clancy's Post Office book were getting smaller and smaller and the time was coming when we'd have to get jobs. We'd both understood that this would happen sooner or later. It wasn't so much the having to work that depressed us, but the thought that this would change us. We wanted to believe we could go out to work and still keep our desert island intact. But we knew, underneath, that work would turn us into the sort of creatures who went to work: puppets who only owned half their lives—and we'd anticipated this by stiffening already and becoming estranged from each other. Maybe this was a sort of defeatism. Clancy started looking at the job columns in newspapers. We'd existed quite happily before without newspapers. It was a sign of how different things were that I'd watch her for some time sitting with the pages spread in front of her, before asking the needless question: "What are you doing?"

"Looking for jobs. What's it look like?"

"If anyone's going to get a job it'll be me," I said, tapping a finger against my chest.

Clancy shook her head. "No," she said, licking a finger to turn over a page, "You've got to perfect your painting. You mustn't give that up, must you?"

She really meant this.

"You're not going out to work while I piss about here," I said, feeling I was adopting a stupid pose.

Then we had a row—Clancy accused me of betraying ideals—the upshot of which was that we both went out the next Monday looking for jobs, feeling mean and demoralised.

There was a dearth of employment, especially for school-leavers. But it was possible to find casual, menial jobs, which was all we wanted. Clancy got a job as a waitress in a pizza house near the Elephant and Castle. I went there once and bought a cup of coffee. She was dressed up in a ridiculous white outfit, with a white stiff cap with a black stripe and her hair pinned up like a nurse. On the walls of the pizza house there were murals with pseudo-Italian motifs which were worse than my pseudo-Gauguins. I looked at Clancy at the service counter and thought of her lying on the bed in the sunshine and swimming in the muddy creek in Suffolk and how she'd said: "Paint me." It was so depressing that when she brought me my coffee we said "Hello" to each other as if we were slight acquaintances.

I got a job in a factory which made lawn-mowers. Bits of lawn-mower came along on moving racks and you had to tighten up the nuts with a machine like a drill on the end of a cable. This was all you did all day. It turned you into an imbecile.

Three or four weeks passed. We'd come in, tired and taciturn after work, and spend the evening getting on each other's nerves. We thought, once we left our jobs behind then we'd return to our own life. But it wasn't like that. We brought our jobs home with us as we brought home the day's sweat in our sticky clothes. Clancy was still serving frothy coffee; I was still tightening nuts. Clancy would slump on the bed and I'd stare out the window. Work seemed a process of humiliation. I looked at the scrap-heaps and demolition sites which once we'd been able to ignore, which we'd even transformed into a landscape of happiness. I thought: We'd escaped, in the midst of everything we'd escaped; but now the tower blocks and demolition sites were closing in. I made an effort to keep cheerful. I read out poems from the book and I explained to Clancy how I was going to finish my mural. But she didn't listen. She no longer seemed to care about my artistic talents. All she seemed interested in were the letters from her uncle, and when one arrived she'd read it over in a lingering, day-dreamy way and not let me look at it. It was as if she were trying to make me jealous.

Once, as I was flipping through *Sonnets and Lyrics*, I came across a poem I hadn't noticed before. "Here," I said, "listen to this." And I read aloud:

Sweet Suffolk owl, so trimly dight,
With feathers like a lady bright . . .

I thought she would like it.

She whipped the book from my hands and flung it across the room. It landed under the sink, near the zinc tub. It was a good, solid book; and it wasn't even mine. I watched the pages come away from the binding at the spine.

"It's crap! All the poems in that book are crap! Artificial, contrived crap!"

She said this with such venom that I believed her at once. A whole reservoir of delight was instantly poisoned.

"Like those paintings," she said, getting up and gesturing. "They're crap too! Sentimental, affected, second-hand crap! They're not even well painted!"

And at once I saw my Tahitian girls—each one a would-be Clancy—for what they really were: stumpy, stick-legged ciphers, like the drawings of a four-year-old.

"Crap, crap! All of it!"

Then she began to cry, and brushed me away when I tried to comfort her.

It was now past the middle of July. Everything was turning bad. Then, to cap matters, I had an accident with a saucepan of boiling water and scalded myself badly.

It happened needlessly and stupidly. The ledge on which our two gas rings rested was only a rickety affair, held up by wall brackets. The plaster below, into which the wall brackets were screwed, was soft and crumbly and we knew there was a danger of the ledge giving way. I kept saying to Clancy I'd fix it. One day we were making kedgeree. Clancy had put the saucepan on to boil for the rice and I was bending down to scrap something into the rubbish box which was just to the left of the gas rings. Clancy suddenly said, "Look out!" A great chunk of plaster had fallen out of the wall and the left hand bracket was hanging on only by the tips of the screws. Instead of doing the sensible thing and jumping out of the way, I reached to hold up the ledge. Just as I did so the bracket came away and most of the contents of the boiling saucepan slopped over my hands.

I did a sort of dance round the room. Clancy yelled at me to put my hands under the tap. "Cold water! It's the best thing!"

she said, trying to keep calm. But although I knew she was quite right, I didn't want to do this at first. I wanted to scream and curse and ignore Clancy and frighten her. It was a kind of revenge for her deriding my painting.

"Fuck! Fuck!" I said, waving my hands and hopping.

"The tap!" said Clancy.

"Shit! Shit!"

The pain was bad at first, but it was nothing to the pain that began about an hour later and went on for hours. By this time I was sitting astride a chair by the sink, my arms plunged into cold water, my forehead pressed against the sink rim, while Clancy kept topping up the water, which would start to steam after a while, and sponged my upper arms. It wasn't pain alone, though that was bad enough. I started to feel shivery and sick—Clancy put a blanket round my shoulders. At the same time we were both silently thinking that perhaps I had a serious scald which needed proper medical treatment. This frightened and dismayed us. It wasn't just that we feared that a visit to a hospital would lay us open to discovery—we were already worried that our jobs might do that. It was more that going to a doctor would be a sort of admission of helplessness. Up till now everything we'd done, even getting jobs, had been done independently, of our own choosing, and hard though things had got, nothing had made us feel we couldn't survive by ourselves.

"I'm scared," Clancy said.

"It's all right. I'll be all right," I said, my face pressed against the wet enamel of the sink. "I shan't go to any doctor."

Clancy sponged my arms.

"I didn't mean it about your painting. Really. And I didn't mean to throw your book at the wall. I was just depressed."

Most of that night we sat like that, I slumped over the sink and Clancy sponging. I was too much in pain to sleep. Whenever I took my hands from the water they felt as if they were being scalded a second time. Clancy tried to say reassuring things and now and then her hand tightened on my shoulder. We listened to the trains clacking up and down and the strange noises of the tenement. Only at about four did we attempt to go to bed, and then Clancy half filled the zinc tub with water and placed it by the bed, so that I lay on one side with my arms dangling into water—though I didn't sleep. Clancy nestled with her arm round me. I felt her doze off very quickly. I thought: In spite of the pain I'm in, in spite of our lousy jobs, in spite of everything, we are happier now, and closer than we've been for several weeks.

In the morning there were huge pearly blisters on my hands. The fingers had mostly escaped unharmed but the palms, the wrists and parts of the backs of the hands were in a hideous state. The pain had eased but the slightest touch or trying to bend my wrists brought it back instantly. Clancy got up, went out to a chemist and came back with various things in tubes and bottles including a thick, slimy cream the colour of beeswax. She made a phone call to her pizza house and gave some excuse about not coming in. The fact was that though I could waggle my fingers I could not close my blistered palms and Clancy had to spoon-feed me and literally be my hands. I knew the important thing with burns was to keep the blistered area free of infection and to let the skin repair by exposure to the air. So for two days we sat, out of the direct sunlight, my hands held out in front of us like a pair of gruesome exhibits, waiting for the blisters to go down. Things were like they were when we'd first run away and got our room.

"Will it leave a scar?" Clancy said.

"Probably," I said.

"I won't mind."

"Good."

"There could be worse places for it."

Even when, on the fourth day, Clancy went back to work (I insisted that she did—I could just hold a spoon by this stage, and I was worried she'd lose her job if she left it any longer), the evenings were somehow special. They were not like the dull, fretful evenings we had had of late. Clancy would come in, her waitress work over, and only want to know about my hands. We discussed them and fussed over them like some third thing which tied us together. It was as if we had a child. As they began to get better we started to make grim, extravagant jokes at their expense:

"The blisters'll burst and pus will go flying all round the room."

"They'll shrivel up into nothing."

"They'll go manky and mouldy and have to be cut off—then you'll be a cripple and I won't love you any more."

I thought: When my hands are better, when I'm no longer an invalid—this happiness will fade.

But though, after a week, my hands were no longer very painful, it was some time—over three weeks—before the skin fully recovered and hardened. Throughout this period I sat idle in the room all day and I noticed, each evening, how Clancy's mood dulled, how she became tired again and begrudging. She saw this herself and tried to resist it. Once she came in with another brown paper parcel. It was a book—*Love Poetry of the Seventeenth Century*. She had made a special trip in her lunch break to get it.

"It can't be much fun sitting here all by yourself all day."

We had moved the bed permanently under the window now, and I used to sit, propped up against the metal bed-head, looking out, like some dying man on a verandah, taking his last view of the world. I thought about lots of things—in between snatches of Herrick and Crashaw—during those long, hot days. Of the lawn-mower factory—someone else would have my job by now and perhaps no one would know I'd ever been there. Of my parents and Clancy's parents; whether they really worried about us or had forgotten us. Of Gauguin dying in Tahiti. And I thought about Clancy's uncle. Clancy hadn't had a letter from him for a while (she usually had one about once a week), and this worried her. I imagined him sitting, just as I was sitting, a cripple, in his wheel-chair in the sunshine. I wondered whether he really did enthuse about Clancy and our running away or whether it was just the foolish, romantic notion of a tired, slightly dotty old man who couldn't move. Perhaps, in his enthusiasm, he merely lied for Clancy's sake, because he was really too sick and worn out to care. I thought about the money that Clancy said he had. I didn't believe in this money. The money of people with big houses in the country always proves to be non-existent. Or it all gets accounted for in debts and duties. In any case, the money made me uneasy. The more I thought, the more suspicious and sceptical I became. I found I couldn't imagine the orchard wall, the creek with the jetty. I even began to believe that Clancy's uncle and his house didn't exist; they were some fiction invented by Clancy as an incentive—like Clancy's father imagining he was descended from the aristocracy.

I read from the book Clancy had bought me—Lovelace, Suckling, the Earl of Rochester—but my attention wandered. I became irritable and sullen. I had to sit with my hands inside a plastic carrier-bag because otherwise flies would come buzzing round settling on my cracked and blistered skin. Every time I wanted to turn a page I had to take out my hands, wave away the flies and use just my finger tips on the book. If I wanted to shift my position I had to do so without using my hands. Simple things became complicated feats. I would sit pondering the absurdity of my position: stuck on a bed with my hands in a polythene bag, reading Lovelace to the sound of bulldozers, half surrounded by the painting (there was still a lot of wall to go) which I was incapable of continuing. And from this I'd leap to wider absurdities. What were we doing in a condemned tenement in Bermondsey? What would become of us in the future?

"You've let the cover curl up in the sun."

Clancy had come in. She had her tired, waitress face.

"I know," I said. "Sorry."

I used to watch the school across the road; the kids coming

and going in the morning and afternoon and streaming into the playground at breaks. It was getting near the time they broke up for the summer; then the school would close for good and the demolition men would move in. Through one of the tall windows, opposite but a little below our room, I could see the teacher standing before the blackboard, but because of the level of the window I couldn't see his seated class. It looked as if he was speaking and gesticulating to no one. I watched him struggling to communicate with his invisible audience, waving his arms and raising his voice, and I felt sorry for him. He made me think of Mr. Boyle, who even now would be offering Sidney and Spenser to the fifth year, who were more interested in Rod Stewart and Charlton Athletic. It seemed ages since I left school, though it was only a year. I thought of all my old school friends and what they were doing, whether they had jobs or not. I thought of Eddy. He'd somehow disowned me as soon as I got interested in poetry. I wondered if there were units of the Royal Artillery in Northern Ireland. I wondered if Eddy was sitting in an armoured car in the Falls Road thinking of Mr. Boyle.

In the third week of July the school closed and the din from the playground ceased. Almost immediately several council vans turned up and took away the interior furnishings. Some of the equipment in the kitchen was dismantled and some old fold-up desks were stacked in the playground. Then the vans drove away, leaving the school like a forlorn fort amidst the besieging demolition sites. I asked myself if the kids who had gone to the school cared that it was going to be flattened. I saw some of them sometimes, playing games over the demolition sites, rooting about amongst the rubbish heaps, setting fire to things and being chased off by the site workers.

Then one day, only about a fortnight after the school closed, there were two boys in the school playground. They were walking around, looking at the heap of desks and peering through the wired ground-floor windows. I was puzzled as to how they'd got there. Then I saw the head of a third boy—and a fourth—appear over the playground wall in the far left corner where it joined the school building. There seemed to be a loose section of the wire netting above the wall, which could be lifted back and squeezed under, and although the wall was a good ten feet, the pile of desks in the corner made it possible, even for a boy of eleven or so, to lower himself down. In a short while there were five boys in the playground, mooching about in grubby jeans and T-shirts.

Their first impulse was to ransack everything. I watched them try to force their way into the school building through the big door from the playground. When this failed, they picked up some old lengths of piping left by the council workers and, poking them through the metal grilles over the windows, began smashing the panes. They used the same bits of piping to hack up lumps of asphalt from the playground, which they hurled at the upper windows. The noise they made was lost in the general noise of demolition. One of them climbed up onto the roof of one of the two small lavatory buildings abutting the school wall and, with the aid of a drain pipe, tried to reach the second-floor windows—but climbed down when he realised he would be visible from street level. Then they started to dismantle the lavatories themselves—crude little temporary buildings made from flimsy prefabricated materials, with corrugated asbestos roofs.

I wondered whether these were the same kids who broke into the tenement and set fire to the litter on the stairs. They came the next day, and the day after that, and the next day again. It seemed odd that they should return at all to the school—like released prisoners going voluntarily back to prison. They stripped the lavatories bare so that the cisterns, bowls and rusty urinals were exposed, and these became the subjects of scatological frenzies. They started to break up some of the desks from the pile in the corner. One day I noticed them throwing about something soft and dark which they had discovered on the asphalt. They were hurling it at each other's faces and laughing. I realised it was a pigeon, a sooty-feathered London pigeon that must have fluttered very recently into the playground to die. They kept tossing it at each other; until one of them picked it up by the wing, raised it high and jerked his arm hard so that the wing came off in his hand. They all laughed. He did the same with the second wing. Then they began a mad, yelling, directionless game of football, kicking the pigeon's body across the asphalt and against the playground walls. The grey lumps of bird turned a dark, purply red. The game ended when one of the boys kicked the bird unintentionally over the playground wall. Nobody seemed interested in retrieving it.

This was on the third afternoon. After the game with the pigeon they grew listless and lethargic. They sat and sprawled about on the broken-up asphalt, now and then gouging up lumps of it and throwing them aimlessly. The sun blazed down. They looked like real prisoners now, idle and demoralized inside the high walls. I thought: They've had enough; they'll go now—their old playground holds nothing for them.

But they didn't go. They re-appeared the next morning. It was as if there had been some over-night resolution. Between them, they had a pick-axe, a shovel and a long-handled fork. Perhaps they had been stolen from one of the building sites. They began to discuss something in the near right-hand corner of the playground, looking at the ground and marking out imaginary lines with their feet. Then one of them lifted the pick-axe and, rather clumsily at first, began hacking at the asphalt. It was difficult to see all this. Even with my high vantage point, the near wall partially obscured them. But it was obvious they were digging a hole. When one had wielded the pick-axe for a few minutes another would take over, and at intervals one of them would scrape away the dislodged asphalt and earth with the shovel. The unoccupied ones sat around, looking on silently and intently.

I wondered what all this meant. By mid-day they had dug a

hole deep enough to come up to their shoulders and there was a substantial heap of earth on the asphalt. Two of them went off and returned later with other tools—trowels, garden forks, a bucket. All of a sudden, I understood. They were digging a tunnel. The hole was perhaps seven or eight feet from the right hand wall. If they dug towards it and for about the same distance beyond it they would emerge in the little triangle of grass—now almost worn away or dried up by the sun—with the solitary bench on it.

I watched them work on all that afternoon and the next morning. They reached the tricky point where they had to turn the angle of the hole so that they could start to dig horizontally towards the wall. Why were they doing it? Was it a game? Had they transformed the playground, in their minds, into some prison camp, patrolled by armed guards and watch-dogs? Their task was too strenuous for a game, surely. And yet, if it wasn't a game, it was absurd: They were trying to escape from a place they had entered—and could leave—at their own free will. Suddenly, I wanted them to succeed.

"Look Clancy—" I said. Clancy had come in from work. She had a carton of yoghurt with her. She sat down, ripped off the foil and began eating without speaking. "—a tunnel."

Clancy looked out of the window. "What tunnel?" All she could see was a pile of earth in the playground.

She licked at her yoghurt, bending her face over it.

"A tunnel. The kids are digging a tunnel in the playground."

"That's a stupid thing to do."

I didn't explain. We didn't talk much to each other in the evenings now. It seemed an effort.

For several days I watched them dig. I forgot my hands, my irritation, my uselessness. From where I sat, I could see the goal of their labours—the patch of grass to the right of the wall—whereas they could not. I surveyed their exertions like a god. But there was much that I couldn't see. I couldn't see how far the tunnel had progressed—all I could see was the expanding heaps of earth and, every few minutes, a boy emerging from the entrance hole, gasping and smeared with soil, and another taking his place. I began to have fears for them. Might the whole thing cave in? Had they dug deep enough to go beneath the foundations of the wall? How were they managing to breathe and to extract the earth as they dug? But now and then I would glimpse things that reassured me: odd bits of wood—fragments of desks and the torn-down lavatories—being used for shoring, lengths of hosepipe, a torch, plastic bags on the ends of cords. On the asphalt over the estimated line of the tunnel they marked out a broad lane in chalk where, clearly, no one was to stand. Their ingenuity, their determination enthralled me. I remembered the pigeon they had kicked round the playground. But I worried about other things that might still thwart them. Might they run into a gas main and be forced to stop? Might they simply give up from exhaustion? And if they overcame all this, might the council men or the demolition workers arrive before they had time to finish? The more I thought of all these things, the more it seemed that their escape was real: that there was a conspiracy of forces against them and some counter-force in the boys themselves.

I did not want to imagine them failing.

I said to Clancy: "My hands will be better soon."

"Oh—really. That's good."

"It could have been worse. Think of all the worse things that could have happened."

"That's right—look on the bright side."

We were quite apart now, wrapped in ourselves. Clancy spent all her time sweating in the pizza house or brooding over her uncle and his absent letters, and I spent all my time obsessed by the tunnel.

It was nearing the middle of August. The sun kept shining. The evening papers Clancy sometimes brought home spoke of droughts and water restrictions. People were complaining of the fine weather. They would have complained just as much if the summer had been wet. On the little triangular plot by the school the thin grass had turned a straw colour and the earth was hard and cracked. I kept watch on this patch of ground now. At any moment I expected the tunnellers to break surface. In the corner of the playground the diggers seemed to be getting excited. The nearer the moment came, the more I exaggerated the dangers of discovery and I willed the council men to delay one more day. I thought of the difficulty of digging up, entombed by earth, against the hard, baked top-soil.

And then, one afternoon, it happened. It seemed odd that it should happen, just like that, without fanfares and announcements. Suddenly, a segment of cracked soil lifted like a lid, only about five feet from the outer face of the wall. A trowel poked upwards, and a hand, and then, after a pause in which the earth lid rocked and crumbled, a head thrust into the air in a cloud of dust. It wore an expression of serene joy as if it had surfaced in a new world. It lay perched for some time on the ground, as if it had no body, panting and grining. Then it let out a cry of triumph. I watched the head drag out shoulders and arms, and a body behind it; and then the four on the other side of the wall disappear one by one into the hole and re-appear, struggling out, on the grass triangle. No one seemed to see them—the traffic went by heedlessly, the bulldozers whined and growled. It was as if they had been transformed and were invisible. They brushed themselves down and—like climbers on a mountain peak—shook each other's hands. And then, they simply ran off—down the adjacent side street, past the boarded up shops and the empty terraces—covered in earth, clasping each other and flinging their fists ecstatically into the air.

Clancy came in about an hour later.

"Clancy," I said, "Clancy, I want to tell you something—" But she was waving an envelope at me, a long white envelope with black print on it. Her face was strangely agitated, as if she might be either pleased or upset.

"Look," she said.

"Clancy, Clancy—"

"Look at this."

She took the letter out of the envelope and placed it in front of me. It bore the heading of a firm of solicitors in Ipswich. The letter began with condolences and mentioned the "sad death" of Clancy's uncle, as if this were something that Clancy should already be aware of, and then went on to speak of "our late client's special and confidential instructions." The gist of it was that Clancy's uncle was dead and Clancy had been left the larger part of his money and property, subject to its being held in trust till she was twenty-one. There were vague, guarded statements about the exact scope of the legacy and a reference to "outstanding settlements," but a meeting with Clancy was sought as soon as possible.

"Well—what do you think?"

"I'm sorry."

"Sorry?"

"Sorry about your uncle."

We looked at each other without speaking. I didn't know what else to say. I took Clancy's hand in my own, half-healed, scabrous hand.

I said: "Clancy, it's your day off tomorrow. Let's go out. Let's go out and get a train to somewhere in the country, and talk."

HOTEL

THE DAY THEY LET ME out of the hospital I went for a long walk round the streets. People looked very remote and sorry for themselves. I noticed there was scarcely anyone who didn't show some sign of strain, of fear, of worry. And I seemed somehow superior to them, as if they were dwarf people and I was bigger and taller and had a better view than they. And, very occasionally, just here and there, there seemed to be other taller, clearer-sighted people who seemed capable, if they wished, of taking charge of all the others, of directing them and consoling them.

Then I went back the next day, as I'd promised, to say goodbye to Dr. Azim, who'd been called away on the day they discharged me. I said to him, "I want to tell you how much I'm grateful for what you've done. And I want to say how much I admire the work of you and your staff." He smiled and looked flattered. I continued my farewell speech. "I see now," I said, "where I went wrong. It's all very clear. You have to be one of those who cares for others rather than one of those whom others care for. It's simple." Then I said, "I've been happy here." And Dr. Azim beamed, and shook hands with me when I left. And I knew then that one day I must occupy some hospitable and protective role like his.

I spent over three months in the hospital, from a time shortly after my mother died. The police picked me up on the street because I was shouting things out loud and alarming passers-by. They thought I was drunk or on some sort of drug. But when they found out neither was the case they took me to see Dr. Azim and his colleagues.

It's strange that I should have been delivered at the hospital doors by the police, because at first so much of what was called my "therapy" seemed to resemble criminal investigation. It was as though I were a suspect and the important thing, to save everyone time and trouble, was for me to make a clean breast of it. The doctors would conduct little question-games, like interrogations, and when I failed to come up with the right answer, they would sigh disappointedly, pump me full of tranquilizers and wait for the next session. I seriously wondered if at a certain stage they would resort to tougher, harsher methods.

So it was a relief to myself as well as them when I said: "The fact is, I wanted to kill my mother."

In one sense I don't think this changed anything. Merely saying it. But my doctors seemed pleased and started to busy themselves on my behalf; and from that day my relations with them changed. They became more friendly, they started to take me, as it were, into their confidence. And from that day too I began to admire them.

Only one thing seemed to disappoint them, and that was the way I failed to give a satisfactory answer to their further question: "Why did you want to kill her? Didn't you love her?"

It was the second part of it that upset me. My first instinct was to be angry with them. I loved her very much. But I saw how this would trap me. So I started to tell them how when my father left us, three years ago, Mother and I had to look after each other. How, considering everything, we were happy, and I was even rather glad (though I didn't tell them this) that Father had gone. And when I got a bit older, I started to get these feelings, hard to explain, that mother wanted to do me harm. I got scared of her and angry with her, and then as the feelings got worse I started to wish she was dead. And then she really did die. She was knocked down in the High Street, by a car which, so they told me, was hardly going at any speed. But she died. I had to go to the hospital to identify her.

Then my doctors said, "But if you were frightened of your mother, if you thought she would do you harm, why didn't you leave her?" I didn't answer that. When things got to this point it would be time for one of my injections.

So I never told them exactly why I wanted to kill Mother, but perhaps what I did tell them gave them plenty to be getting on with, because, as I say, our relations improved. We would often talk about my "problem" as if we were talking about some third person who was not present. I stopped having my gabbling and shouting fits, or my sessions of weeping inconsolably because of my dead mother. I was told by Dr. Azim, who had taken charge of my case, that I was making progress. And I agreed.

Once I said to Dr. Azim: "So is that what it amounts to? I've been put in here—people think I'm mad—because I wished to kill my mother?"

Dr. Azim smiled and gave an expression which suggested that this was taking a naive view.

"No, it's not your wish to kill your mother that's brought you here. It's your guilt about that wish."

So I said to him: "Does that mean then that the answer would be to have your wish."

He smiled again. He had a reassuring smile.

"It's not as simple as that. There are wishes, and there are wishes..."

Then there followed a period of five or six weeks—which I still look upon as one of the sweetest in my life—when, with my main course of therapy over, I was required only to recover slowly, like any convalescent after an illness. It was summer and I spent a lot of time sitting on the hospital lawns, observing the other patients, talking to Dr. Azim, and thinking about this business of guilt and secret wishes.

It seems to me that there can scarcely be anyone walking the earth who doesn't carry with him some measure of guilt; and that guilt is always the sign of some forbidden happiness. Somewhere inside everybody's guilt is joy, and somewhere within everybody's unhappy, guilt-ridden face is happiness. Perhaps there's no way out of this. And yet there must be someone who will try to understand our guilt and not blame it; there must be places where we can go where our secret wishes can be uttered and our forbidden dreams catered for. There must, in a word, be care.

And then I felt privileged to be where I was, and very proud to have met Dr. Azim and his colleagues; and I had the feeling that perhaps every recovering inmate experiences, of being an honoured and fortunate guest. So perhaps it was then, and before that first walk out of the hospital gates, that the ambition was sown in me that would one day make me a hotel-keeper.

But don't think I walked out of that hospital with a worked-out plan for something which, of course, was then quite beyond my reach. My efforts matured slowly. For many years I ran a small café, bought with the money mother left me—no different from countless other cafés. I made a point of getting to know my customers, of making them feel that they could talk to me and I would listen; and some of them appreciated this, though some of them took exception and never came back.

Don't think, either, that a lot of time didn't pass and a lot of living didn't get done between the day I left the hospital and the day I opened my hotel. I got married. My wife helped me with the café and even put her money towards it. It's true, our marriage didn't work out. It wasn't happy. But I'd learnt to take a balanced view of unhappiness. My wife—Carol—often told me that I treated her like a child; I patronised her, talking down to her. The strange thing was it seemed to me to be the other way round.

When we got divorced, I decided not to marry again. I bought a new café in a nicer suburb with rooms above it so it could be used as a guest-house. For a long time—until it began to pay—I ran this virtually single-handedly, which was hard work. But I was good at it. I had a natural flair, I'd discovered, for catering—cooking, making beds, attending to laundry—I'd learnt it in those years with Mother. I don't think I was ever lonely, not having a wife. You're never lonely in the café and guest-house business, with people to look after. After a while I could afford a couple of permanent staff, and this enabled me to take the odd half-day off—to visit Mother's grave, to go to look up Dr. Azim, though I was saddened to learn that he had retired through ill-health, and his whereabouts were unknown.

So many years went by, dull, if busy, years on the face of it. But I always felt I was only waiting, marking time. My ambition of a hotel was crystallizing. And I knew there would come a time when that long period—over thirty years in all—between my leaving the hospital and owning my hotel would seem unimportant, a preparation, a mere journey between two points.

Because you see, if I haven't made it clear already, my idea of a hotel wasn't just the crowning of a career in catering, the next step up from high street café and small-time guest-house. It was a genuine idea. I had no interest in providing mere board and lodging, though, God knows, I could provide that. I wanted a hotel that would be like my old hospital without its department of health notices. A hotel—of happiness.

And at last, after waiting, saving and searching, I found it: a twelve-bedroomed establishment in a west country town, beside a river. The former proprietors, local people, seemed to have lacked imagination and failed to see its potential. Within five years I had transformed it into a haven where people came, summer and winter, for what I used to call—and many of my guests were taken by the phrase—"therapeutic visits." I think it owed some of its success—which is not to be modest—to the presence of water. The restaurant looked out across a lawn with white painted chairs and tables to the river, and there was not a room in the building in which could not be heard the soft rushing of a nearby weir. People like to be near water. It gives them a feeling of being cleansed, of being purified.

But there are plenty of small hotels beside rivers in pleasant country towns, and these things alone don't explain the special charm my hotel had. I still like to believe it had a special charm. I like to believe that when people stepped through the entrance of my hotel they felt at once they were in the hands of someone who cared. Somehow I knew that "out there," in the lives they came from, there were all kinds of things—guilty things—that they would be reluctant to admit to and came to escape from. And somehow they knew that I knew this and that I understood and didn't blame or condemn. And in the meantime I offered them a week, a fortnight, of release. When I talked to them—because I always tried to get my guests to speak—they would sometimes laugh over matters that before, I am sure, they might have cried about or not dared to broach, and this atmosphere of candour, of amnesty, was all part of the cure.

Of course, there are always those who don't want to talk and give away nothing. But faces show things. People always smiled in my hotel, even if they checked in with tired and reticent expressions. And if all this isn't proof enough, I only have to quote the list of guests who returned to my hotel over and over again, sometimes several times in the same year, or the affidavits of those who wrote to me personally to say how much they enjoyed their stays. A lot of these people, I don't mind admitting, had money and influence. But that isn't the important thing. The important thing is that they were grateful to me, they were loyal to me, they appreciated what I was doing.

And I mustn't omit to mention that special category of guests for whom I always catered with particular delicacy and for whom my hotel was the very scene of their guiltiness—and their happiness. I mean the couples—the lovers—who turned up without booking or at short notice and signed themselves in, if not as Mr. and Mrs. Smith, then as Mr. and Mrs. Jones or Mr. and Mrs. Kilroy. Never for one moment did I allow them to feel unwelcome. Instead I let them understand in all sorts of subtle ways, that I saw through them yet permitted—blessed—their subterfuge. So that as I directed them to their rooms it was as though I were saying, "Go on—have your wish, have your forbidden joy." And I like to think that in my hotel rooms, to the sound of the purring weir, they did indeed find their secret bliss.

My other guests—I mean my respectably married or unattached guests—were not upset by the presence—if they detected it—of these illicit lovers in their midst. Far from it. They either pretended not to notice or they winked at it—literally sometimes—with a kind of vicarious pleasure. It was as though they were relieved, exonerated in some way by what was going on, perhaps in the very next room to theirs. And the reason for this is that we are all guilty.

You see, there was nothing stuffy and stuck-up about my hotel, as there is about so many country hotels. In my hotel all was forgiven.

And all this went on for many years. My guests sat in the restaurant or at the white tables under the sun-umbrellas. They watched the river rippling by; they wined and dined; they went for their walks and their fishing; they bought antiques in the town; they smiled and knew they were well looked after; and they wrote letters, to thank me and said they would come again.

Until one day a couple checked in who were different from

the others. Not obviously and immediately different: the man in his forties, the girl heavily made up and a lot younger, perhaps still in her teens—which made their purpose in wanting a room transparent. But this didn't set them apart from all the other couples whose purpose was the same. What struck me was that their faces were more than usually guarded, more than usually strained and marked by frowns, compared with most guests when they first step into my entrance hall. I said to myself, those faces will smile tomorrow. And I ushered them to room eleven.

But they never did smile, their expressions never lightened. That was the first thing that worried me. And their melancholy was only made more noticeable by the way they deliberately avoided other guests, kept to their room for long periods and ate their meals at the least busy times at out-of-the-way tables.

I thought: What can I do for them? How can I help?

And then, on their third morning, when they were eating breakfast in an almost deserted dining-room, one of my chambermaids, who was having her morning coffee, drew me aside at the bar and said, "Look carefully at that girl."

This had to be done circumspectly and partly with the aid of the mirrors behind the bar; but I thought I knew, from my own observations already, what the chambermaid was driving at, and so I said to her quietly, with a shrug and a touch of rebuke for her curiosity, "She's a lot younger than she's trying to make out."

"She can hardly be sixteen. Now keep looking—and look at him as well."

So I kept looking. And when I made no comment my chambermaid said, "I'll lay you ten to one that man is that girl's father."

I don't know why I didn't see it—or believe it—when I spend so much time watching the faces of my guests. I don't know why I replied to my chambermaid, "Nonsense." And I don't know why from that moment on I began to feel threatened and ill at ease in my own hotel. Chambermaids are tolerant, broad-minded people—they have to be in their job—but that chambermaid began to look at me with reproach, as if I were somehow failing in a duty, and if I didn't do something she would take the law into her own hands.

And it wasn't just the chambermaids and other people on my staff. It was the guests. Gossip must have been going around. They began to give me searching, doubting looks, as if they too expected me to do something. But I still didn't see it. All I saw was this couple whose faces seemed so desolate and inconsolable in my hotel of happiness. I wanted to talk to them, to draw them out, but somehow I lacked my usual knack for this, and I was aware that if I did talk to them, in a friendly fashion, I would antagonize everyone else. I watched their unsmiling faces, and in watching their faces I was slow to notice that the smiles on the faces of my other guests were disappearing.

For so they were. It was as if some infection was spreading. The smiles had changed to looks of accusation. But I still didn't see it. One morning, the Russells, a couple who stayed with me many times and were booked for another four days, came down the stairs with their suitcases and requested their bill. When I asked what was wrong they looked at me in disbelief. And the Russells' departure seemed to be a signal for others. A family with young children left; Major Curtis, who came for the fishing, left. They muttered words like "unwholesome" and "fetch the police." Another couple announced: "Either they go or we go."

And then it was clear to me. These people whom I went to such lengths to care for, they weren't in need of care at all. These people who arrived with guilty faces, to have their guilt absolved and their frowns turned to smiles—they weren't guilty at all. They didn't need happiness. They were only people enjoying country air, good food and being away from it all. That was what made them smile. And thrown in amongst them were a few weekend adulterers—bosses with their secretaries, husbands having fun away from their wives. And I had done so much for them—and now they were deserting me.

At that point I stopped feeling concerned for the couple in room eleven. I was furious with that couple. I saw it all right—I'd seen it all along. That couple in room eleven were father and daughter, it was plain as plain, and they had come to my hotel to share the same bed and they were driving all my guests—my precious guests—away. I had to send them packing.

My staff, some of whom had seemed ready to leave as well, rallied round me now that they saw I was about to act. It was the morning of the couple's fifth day at my hotel. I would have to speak to the man, as the—responsible party. My chambermaid had told me that every morning before they came down to breakfast—never earlier than nine-thirty—the girl took a bath in the bathroom on the landing (alas, not all my rooms had private baths) while the man remained in the room. This would be the best time to confront him.

At about nine the chambermaid informed me that the bathroom was occupied and the bath running. I wasn't sure what I was going to say. I'd half prepared openings like "You must leave at once—I think you know why" or "You must leave at once—can't you see what you're doing to my business?"—but after that, what I felt I should say only got blurred and angry. I went up the stairs to number eleven. I was about to knock, loudly, on the door, but in the circumstances I dispensed with propriety, and opened it directly.

I'd expected, of course, to find the man. But they must have changed their routine with the bathroom that morning because I found the girl. The daughter. She was sitting at the dressing-table in a white nightdress with small pink flowers on it. She didn't have her heavy make-up on; perhaps she was about to apply it. She looked incongruous in this position, like a child sitting before a grand piano. You see, she couldn't have been more than fifteen. For the briefest instant she must have thought that I was her father, because when she looked up I got the impression of a cloud suddenly crossing a perfectly clear and peaceful face—as if I might have seen her for a fraction of a second without that habitual look of strain she wore in the public rooms of the hotel. I didn't say anything because I couldn't. I looked into that face. I have never seen a face which looked so guilty and so terrified. But it seemed to me that deep in that face, deep beneath its desperate surface, I saw happiness. It was like the glint of still water at the bottom of a dark well, like a beautiful, long-submerged memory. Just for one moment I thought I could put my hands on that girl's neck and throttle her. A window was open and I could hear the weir.

Then I went down to my hotel office, shut the door and wept.

SERAGLIO

IN ISTANBUL THERE ARE TOMBS, faced with calligraphic designs, where the dead Sultan rests among the tiny catafalques of younger brothers whom he was obliged, by custom, to murder on his accession. Beauty becomes callous when it is set beside savagery. In the grounds of the Topkapi palace the tourists admire the turquoise tiles of the Harem, the Kiosks of the Sultans, and think of girls with sherbet, turbans, cushions, fountains. "So were they just kept here?" my wife asks. I read from the guide-book: "Though the Sultans kept theoretical power over the Harem, by the end of the sixteenth century these women effectively dominated the Sultans."

It is cold. A chill wind blows from the Bosphorus. We had come on our trip in late March, expecting sunshine and mild heat, and found bright days rent by squalls and hail-storms. When it rains in Istanbul the narrow streets below the Bazaar become torrents, impossible to walk through, on which one expects to see, floating with the debris of the market, dead rats, bloated dogs, the washed up corpses of centuries. The Bazaar itself is a labyrinth with a history of fires. People have entered, they say, and not emerged.

From the grounds of the Topkapi the skyline of the city, like an array of upturned shields and spears, is unreal. The tourists murmur, pass on. Turbans, fountains; the quarters of the Eunuchs; the Pavilion of the Holy Mantle. Images out of the *Arabian Nights*. Then one discovers, as if stumbling oneself on the scene of the crime, in a glass case in a museum of robes, the spattered kaftan in which Sultan Oman II was assassinated. Rent by dagger thrusts from shoulder to hip. The thin linen fabric could be the corpse itself. The simple white garment, like a bathrobe, the blood-stains, like the brown stains on the gauze of a removed elastoplast, give you the momentary illusion that it is your gown lying there, lent to another, who is murdered in mistake for yourself.

We leave, towards the Blue Mosque, through the Imperial Gate, past the fountain of the Executioner. City of monuments and murder, in which cruelty seems ignored. There are cripples in the streets near the Bazaar, shuffling on leather pads, whom the tourists notice but the inhabitants do not. City of siege and massacre and magnificence. When Mehmet the Conqueror captured it in 1453 he gave it over to his men, as was the custom, for three days of pillage and slaughter; then set about building new monuments. These things are in the travel books. The English-speaking guides, not using their own language, tell them as if they had never happened. There are miniatures of Mehmet in the Topkapi Museum. A pale, smooth-skinned man, a patron of the arts, with a sensitive gaze and delicate eyebrows, holding a rose to his nostrils...

It was after I had been explaining to my wife from the guide-book, over lunch in a restaurant, about Mehmet's rebuilding of the city, that we walked round a corner and saw a taxi—one of those metallic green taxis with black and yellow chequers down the side which cruise round Istanbul like turquoise sharks—drive with almost deliberate casualness into the legs of a man pushing a cart by the kerb. A slight crunch; the man fell, his legs at odd angles, clothes torn, and did not get up. Such things should not happen on holiday. They happen at home—people cluster round and stare—and you accommodate it because you know ordinary life includes such things. On holiday you want to be spared ordinary life.

But then it was not the fact of the accident for which we were unprepared but the reactions of the involved parties. The injured man looked as if he were to blame for having been injured. The taxi driver remained in his car as if his path had been deliberately blocked. People stopped on the pavement and gabbled, but seemed to be talking about something else. A policeman crossed from a traffic island. He had dark glasses and a peaked cap. The taxi driver got out of his car. They spoke languidly to each other and seemed both to have decided to ignore the man on the road. Beneath his dark glasses the policeman's lips moved delicately and almost with a smile, as if he were smelling a flower. We walked on round the corner. I said to my wife, even though I knew she would disapprove of the joke: "That's why there are so many cripples."

Our hotel is in the new part of Istanbul, near the Hilton, overlooking the Bosphorus, across which there is a newly built bridge. Standing on the balcony you can look from Europe to Asia. Uskudar, on the other side, is associated with Florence Nightingale. There are few places in the world where, poised on one continent, you can gaze over a strip of water at another.

We had wanted something more exotic. No more Alpine chalets and villas in Spain. We needed yet another holiday, but a different holiday. We had had this need for eight years and it was a need we could afford. We felt we had suffered in the past and so required a perpetual convalescence. But this meant, in time, even our holidays lacked novelty; so we looked for somewhere more exotic. We thought of the East. We imagined a landscape of minarets and domes out of the *Arabian Nights*. However, I pointed out the political uncertainties of the Middle East to my wife. She is sensitive to such things, to even remote hints of calamity. In London bombs go off in the Hilton and restaurants in Mayfair. Because she has borne one disaster she feels she should be spared all others, and she looks upon me to be her guide in this.

"Well Turkey then—Istanbul," she said—we had the brochures open on the table, with their photographs of the Blue Mosque—"that's not the Middle East." I remarked (facetiously perhaps: I make these digs at my wife and she appreciates them for they reassure her that she is not being treated like something fragile) that the Turks made trouble too; they had invaded Cyprus.

"Don't you remember the Hamiltons' villa? They're still waiting to know what's become of it."

"But we're not going to Cyprus," she said. And then, looking at the brochure—as if her adventurousness were being tested and she recognised its limits: "Besides, Istanbul is in Europe."

My wife is beautiful. She has a smooth, flawless complexion, subtle, curiously expressive eyebrows, and a slender figure. I think these were the things which made me want to marry her, but though they have preserved themselves well in eight years they no longer have the force of a motive. She looks best in very dark or very pale colours. She is fastidious about perfumes, and tends devotedly our garden in Surrey.

She is lying now on the bed in our hotel bedroom in Istanbul from which you can see Asia, and she is crying. She is crying because while I have been out taking photos, in the morning light, of the Bosphorus, something has happened—she has been interfered with in some way—between her and one of the hotel porters.

I sit down beside her. I do not know exactly what has happened. It is difficult to elicit details while she is crying. However, I am thinking: She only started to cry when I asked, "What's wrong?" When I came into the room she was not crying, only sitting stiller and paler than usual. This seems to me like a kind of obstructiveness.

"We must get the manager," I say, getting up, "the police even." I say this bluffly, even a little heartlessly; partly because I believe my wife may be dramatising, exaggerating (she has been moody, touchy ever since that accident we witnessed: perhaps she is blowing up some small thing, a mistake, nothing at all); partly because I know that if my wife had come out with me to take photos and not remained alone none of this would have occurred; but partly too because as I stare down at her and mention the police, I want her to think of the policeman with his dark glasses and his half-smiling lips and the man with his legs crooked on the road. I see that she does so by the wounded look she gives me. This wounds me in return for having caused it. But I had wanted this too.

"No," she says, shaking her head, still sobbing. I see that she is not sobered by my remark. Perhaps there is something there. She wants to accuse me, with her look, of being cold and sensible and wanting to pass the matter on, of not caring for her distress itself.

"But you won't tell me exactly what happened," I say, as if I am being unfairly treated.

She reaches for her handkerchief and blows her nose deliberately. When my wife cries or laughs her eyebrows form little waves. While her face is buried in the handkerchief I look up out of the window. A mosque on the Asian side, its minarets like thin blades, is visible on the skyline. With the morning light behind it, it seems illusory, like a cut-out. I try to recall its name from the guide-book but cannot. I look back at my wife. She has removed the handkerchief from her eyes. I realise she is right in reproaching me for my callousness. But this process of being harsh towards my wife's suffering, as if I blamed her for it, so that I in turn will feel to blame and she will then feel justified in pleading her suffering, is familiar. It is the only way in which we begin to speak freely.

She is about to tell me what happened now. She crushes the handkerchief in her hand. I realise I really have been behaving as if nothing had happened.

When I married my wife I had just landed a highly sought-after job. I am a consultant designer. I had everything and, I told myself, I was in love. In order to prove this to myself I had an affair, six months after my marriage, with a girl I did not love. We made love in hotels. In the West there are no harems. Perhaps my wife found out or guessed what had happened, but she gave no sign and I betrayed nothing. I wonder whether if a person does not know something has happened it is the same as if nothing had happened. My affair did not affect in any way the happiness I felt in my marriage. My wife became pregnant. I was glad of this. I stopped seeing the girl. Then some months later my wife had a miscarriage. She not only lost the baby, but could not have children again.

I blamed her for the miscarriage. I thought, quite without reason, that this was an extreme and unfair means of revenge. But this was only on the surface. I blamed my wife because I knew that, having suffered herself without reason, she wanted to be blamed for it. This is something I understand. And I blamed my wife because I myself felt to blame for what had happened and if I blamed my wife, unjustly, she could then accuse me, and I would feel guilty, as you should when you are to blame. Also I felt that by wronging my wife, by hurting her when she had been hurt already, I would be driven by my remorse to do exactly what was needed in the circumstances: to love her. It was at this time that I realised that my wife's eyebrows had the same attractions as Arabic calligraphy. The truth was we were both crushed by our misfortune, and by hurting each other, shifting the real pain, we protected each other. So I blamed my wife in order to make myself feel bound towards her. Men want power over women in order to be able to let women take this power from them.

This was seven years ago. I do not know if these reactions have ever ceased. Because we could have no children we made up for it in other ways. We began to take frequent and expensive holidays. We would say as we planned them, to convince ourselves: "We need a break, we need to get away." We went out a lot, to restaurants, concerts, cinemas, theatres. We were keen on the arts. We would go to all the new things, but we would seldom discuss, after seeing a play for instance, what we had watched. Because we had no children we could afford this; but if we had had children we could still have afforded it; since as my career advanced my job brought in more.

This became our story: our loss and its recompense. We felt we had justifications, an account of ourselves. As a result we lived on quite neutral terms with each other. For long periods, especially during those weeks before we took a holiday, we seldom made love—or when we did we would do so as if in fact we were not making love at all. We would lie in our bed, close but not touching, like two continents, each with its own customs and history, between which there is no bridge. We turned our backs towards each other as if we were both waiting our moment, hiding a dagger in our hands. But in order for the dagger thrust to be made, history must first stop, the gap between continents must be crossed. So we would lie, unmoving. And the only stroke, the only wound either of us inflicted was when one would turn and touch the other with empty, gentle hands, as though to say, "See, I have no dagger."

It seemed we went on holiday in order to make love, to stimulate passion (I dreamt, perhaps, long before we actually travelled there, and even though my wife's milky body lay beside me, of the sensuous, uninhibited East). But although our holidays seldom had this effect and were only a kind of make-believe, we did not admit this to each other. We were not like real people. We were like characters in a detective novel. The mystery to be solved in our novel was who killed our baby. But as soon as the murderer was discovered he would kill his discoverer. So the discovery was always avoided. Yet the story had to go on. And this, like all stories, kept us from pain as well as boredom.

"It was the boy—I mean the porter. You know, the one who works on this floor."

My wife has stopped crying. She is lying on the bed. She wears a dark skirt; her legs are creamy. I know who she is talking about, have half guessed it before she spoke. I have seen him, in a white jacket, collecting laundry and doing jobs in the corridor: one of those thick-faced, crop-haired, rather melancholy-looking young Turks with whom Istanbul abounds and who seem either to have just left or to be about to be conscripted into the army.

"He knocked and came in. He'd come to repair the heater. You know, we complained it was cold at night. He had tools. I went out onto the balcony. When he finished he called out something and I came in. Then he came up to me—and touched me."

"Touched you? What do you mean—touched you?" I know my wife will not like my inquisitorial tone. I wonder whether she is wondering if in some way I suspect her behaviour.

"Oh, you know," she says exasperatedly.

"No. It's important I know exactly what happened, if we're—"

"If what?"

She looks at me, her eyebrows wavering.

I realise again that though I am demanding an explanation I really don't want to know what actually happened or, on the other hand, to accept a story. Whether, for example, the Turk touched my wife at all; whether if he did touch her, he only touched her or actually assaulted her in some way, whether my wife evaded, resisted or even encouraged his advances. All these things seem possible. But I do not want to know them. That is why I pretend to want to know them. I see too that my wife does not want to tell me either what really happened or a story. I realise that for eight years, night after night, we have been telling each other the story of our love.

"Well?" I insist.

My wife sits up on the bed. She holds one hand, closed, to her throat. She has this way of seeming to draw in, chastely, the collar of her blouse, even when she is not wearing a blouse or her neck is bare. It started when we lost our baby. It is a way of signalling that she has certain inviolable zones that mustn't be trespassed on. She gets up and walks around the room. She seems overwhelmed and avoids looking out of the window.

"He is probably still out there, lurking in the corridor," she says as if under siege.

She looks at me expectantly, but cautiously. She is not interested in facts but reactions. I should be angry at the Turk, or she should be angry at me for not being angry at the Turk. The truth is we are trying to make each other angry with each other. We are using the incident to show that we have lost patience with each other.

"Then we must get the manager," I repeat.

Her expression becomes scornful, as if I am evading the issue.

"You know what will happen if we tell the manager," she says. "He will smile and shrug his shoulders."

I somehow find this quite credible and for this reason want to scoff at it harshly. The manager is a bulky, balding man, with stylish cuff-links and a long, aquiline nose with sensitive nostrils. Every time trips have been arranged for us which have gone wrong or information been given which has proved faulty he has smiled at our complaints and shrugged. He introduces himself to foreign guests as Mehmet, but this is not significant since every second Turk is a Mehmet or Ahmet. I have a picture of him listening to this fresh grievance and raising his hands, palms exposed, as if to show he has no dagger.

My wife stares at me. I feel I am in her power. I know she is right; that this is not a matter for the authorities. I look out of the window. The sun is glinting on the Bosphorus from behind dark soot-falls of approaching rain. I think of what you read in the guide-books, the *Arabian Nights*. I should go out and murder this Turk who is hiding in the linen cupboard.

"It's the manager's responsibility," I say.

She jerks her head aside at this.

"There'd be no point in seeing the manager," she says.

I turn from the window.

"So actually nothing happened?"

She looks at me as if I have assaulted her.

We both pace about the room. She clasps her arms as if she is cold. Outside the sky is dark. We seem to be entering a labyrinth.

"I want to get away," she says, crossing her arms so her hands are on her shoulders. "This place"—she gestures towards the window. "I want to go home."

Her skin seems thin and luminous in the fading light.

I am trying to gauge my wife. I am somehow afraid she is in real danger. All right, if you feel that bad, I think. But I say, with almost deliberate casualness: "That would spoil the holiday, wouldn't it?" What I really think is that my wife should go and I should remain, in this unreal world where, if I had the right sort of dagger, I would use it on myself.

"But we'll go if you feel that bad," I say.

Outside a heavy shower has begun to fall.

"I'm glad I got those photos then," I say. I go to the window where I have put the guide-books on the sill. A curtain of rain veils Asia from Europe. I feel I am to blame for the weather. I explain from the guide-book the places we have not yet visited.

Exotic names. I feel the radiator under the window ledge. It is distinctly warmer.

My wife sits down on the bed. She leans forward so that her hair covers her face. She is holding her stomach like someone who has been wounded.

The best way to leave Istanbul must be by ship. So you can lean at the stern and watch that fabulous skyline slowly recede, become merely two-dimensional; that *Arabian Nights* mirage which when you get close to it turns into a labyrinth. Glinting under the sun of Asia, silhouetted by the sun of Europe. The view from the air in a Turkish Airlines Boeing, when you have had to cancel your flight and book another at short notice, is less fantastic but still memorable. I look out of the porthole. I am somehow in love with this beautiful city in which you do not feel safe. My wife does not look; she opens a magazine. She is wearing a pale-coloured suit. Other people in the plane glance at her.

All stories are told, like this one, looking back at painful places which have become silhouettes, or looking forward, before you arrive, at scintillating façades which have yet to reveal their dagger thrusts, their hands in hotel bedrooms. They buy the reprieve, or the stay of execution, of distance. London looked inviting from the air, spread out under clear spring sunshine; and one understood the pleasures of tourists staying in hotels in Mayfair, walking in the morning with their cameras and guide-books, past monuments and statues, under plane trees, to see the soldiers at the Palace. One wants the moment of the story to go on for ever, the poise of parting or arriving to be everlasting. So one doesn't have to cross to the other continent, doesn't have to know what really happened, doesn't have to meet the waiting blade.

THE SON

IT'S TRUE: EVERYTHING CHANGES. WHAT you think you know, you don't know. What's good or bad at one time isn't good or bad at another. Once I cut off the fingers of my own mother. You don't believe me? It was during the war in Athens. She was dead. She was dead because there was nothing to eat. And we younger ones were too conscious of our own empty bellies to waste time grieving. There were three fat rings on Mama's fingers—rings to barter for food. But Mama's knuckles were swollen and you couldn't get the rings off by pulling. So, because I was the oldest and expected to make decisions, I got hold of the bread knife...

Thirty-five years ago I chopped off the fingers of my own mother. And now I chop onions in a restaurant. I don't like the way the world's going. Thirty-five years ago the Germans killed Greeks for no reason at all, cut off their hands and put out their eyes. And now, every summer, they flock to Greece in the thousands, take snap-shots of the white houses and the smiling men on donkeys and suffer from sun-burn.

But it's Adoni who tells me about the Germans and their cameras. How should I know about Greece? I haven't been there for thirty years.

What do you do when your country is in ruins, when a war's robbed you of a father, then a mother, and of a nice future all lined up for you in the family business? You do what any Greek does. You find a wife who'll go halves with you; you get on a boat to New York or England, where you're going to open a restaurant. In five or ten years, you say, when you've made your pile, you'll go back to Greece. Twenty years later, when you've only just saved enough money to open that restaurant, and you know there's no money in restaurants anyway, you wake up to the fact that you're never going to go back. Even if you were offered the chance you wouldn't take it.

Yes, I want sunshine. I'm a Greek. What am I doing in the Caledonian Road? I should be sitting in one of the big, noisy cafés on Stadiou or Ermou, clicking my beads and reading *To Vima*. But that's how it is: You're made for one soil, but you put down roots in another and then you can't budge.

And why do I say "Greek"? There are Greeks and Greeks. I was born in Smyrna in Asia Minor. When I was a tiny baby, only a few months old, I was bundled with my parents onto a French ship, because another bunch of butchers, not the Germans this time but the Turks, were burning Greek houses and lopping off the heads of any Greeks they could catch.

Yes, that's the way it is: We're born in confusion and that's how we live.

I can hear Anna clattering in the kitchen below. She's talking to Adoni just as if nothing has happened, everything's the same. It's funny how women can make changes; it's men who are obstinate. "Go and lie down, *Kostaki mou*," she says. "You're tired. Leave the clearing up to Adoni and me." And so I climb the stairs, take off my shoes, my trousers and shirt and lie down in the cramped bedroom from which we can never quite get rid of the smell of food—just as I do every day for a half hour or so between when we shut after lunch and when we open again in the evening. But, today, a little longer.

Tired. Why shouldn't I be tired? Yesterday—what a day!—I had to get up early to meet Adoni at the airport. Then we didn't get to bed till nearly three in the morning. And then, these last two weeks, I've had to work extra hard because Adoni suddenly takes it into head to have a holiday. In Greece. After thirty-five years, he wants to have a holiday.

Adoni, Adoni. Who could have given him that name that sounds so preposterous in English? Adonis. It wasn't us who gave it him. Though Adoni was none the wiser. Adonis Alexopoulos, son of Kosta and Anna; born, Athens, 1944; and carried away by his parents—just as I was carried away from Smyrna—to a new land. How was he to know that his real father was in some mass grave in Poland and his mother had died bringing him into the world? He was taken in by Anna's family, who lived only a block away from us in Kasseveti Street and just a stone's throw from where Adoni's real parents—whose name was Melianos—had lived. Anna said when we got married we'd adopt Adoni as our own son. I wasn't sure if what she meant was: If you want me, then you'll have to take Adoni too. But I agreed. I thought: All right, Anna can have Adoni and sooner or later I'll get a real son of my own. But what Anna never told me was that she couldn't have babies. She was an only daughter and all four of her would-be brothers had been still-born monsters.

What a shameful thing for a man to live thirty-five years not knowing that his parents are not his parents at all. But what a worse shame for a man to have to be told. We always said: When he is old enough we will tell him. But "old enough" always seemed to be just a little bit older. What you put off starts to become impossible. We even began to kid ourselves: He really is ours; he isn't anybody else's.

Perhaps there's a curse on adopted children. Perhaps the fact that they don't have any real parents comes out, not consciously, but in the sort of stunted way they grow up. What did he become, this Adonis of ours? Slow at school, bashful with the other kids; silent; secretive. Every year we waited for him to bloom like a little flower. We said to ourselves: One day he will start chasing the girls; one day he will stay out at night and not come home till late; one day he will stand up and row with his father and say, I want nothing to do with this crazy idea of opening a restaurant, and slam the door on us. I actually wanted these things to happen, because that's how real sons behave with their fathers.

But none of it happened. At eighteen, when we buy the restaurant, and when he's still as chaste and sober as a monk, he puts on a waiter's jacket without so much as a murmur. He learns to cook *dolmades* and *soudsoukakia*. He gets up early every morning to clean up from the night before and to go and order meat and vegetables, and when he does this he doesn't swop jokes with the traders, he simply sticks out a big, podgy finger at what he wants. In the evenings, he doesn't prance and scurry like a waiter should; he lumbers between the tables like a great bear. For even in appearance this Adonis is a rebel to his name. His flesh is pale and pasty; at thirty-five he has the thick build of a man twenty years older. When I make introductions to some of my more enthusiastic customers, when I say, like a proud Greek restaurant owner should, "This is my wife Anna, and this is my son Adonis" (for I've told that lie to half of Camden), I see a snigger cross their faces because the name is so absurd.

"Adonaki," I tell him, "try to use a little charm—you know, charm." But it's no use trying to make that pudding face sparkle.

I shouldn't complain: he works hard; he doesn't spill food or make mistakes over the bills; he pulls corks out of bottles as if he's plucking feathers. And I'm the one who, over the years, has learnt to provide charm. In the evening I'm all smiles. I joke with my customers; I put a sprig of herbs behind my ear—so I can imagine them saying about me: That Kosta in the restaurant, he's a character. And even though I lie in bed in the afternoon, in my yellowed vest, like a great lump of dough, yet, come opening time, I never fail to play my part and give a twinkle to my eyes. We Greeks are like that: We come alive, we perform, like drooping flowers splashed with water.

Anna is coming up the stairs. The stair-case creaks. She is heavier even than me. She'll take her lie-down. But Adoni won't lie down. He'll sit in the restaurant with his feet up on one of the chairs, smoke a cigarette and read the newspaper or one of his books from the library—*Mysteries of the Past, The Secret of Mind-Power*—slowly and methodically. Though he's slow, he likes asking questions, that boy. And he finds out the answers. Oh yes. Give him time, he'll find out about everything.

Anna waddles into the bedroom. I pretend that I'm asleep, though I watch her with one half-closed eye. She kicks off her shoes, then her fat arms grope to undo her dress. It falls off her without her having to help it, like a monument being unveiled. In her slip she is like a huge pale blancmange inside a white, diaphanous wrapping. She shuffles around to her side of the bed, winds and sets the alarm-clock. She always does this in case we oversleep. But I've never known a time when she wasn't awake and heaving herself onto her feet without the alarm having to remind her. She's like that: She does what has to be done. That vast body of hers is built for sweating in the kitchen and scrubbing pans. We men, we like our fancies, our bit of hot spice in a skirt, but where would we be without these great work-horses to pull us through?

She settles down next to me and she sees that I'm not really asleep. I open my eyes. "It doesn't matter, Kostaki," she says. "It doesn't matter. Who are we anyway?"

Her body smells of warm grease and scouring powder. How can it be that that womb of hers—which can now produce nothing—would have once produced not men but deformities? How can it be that she has grown into this vast flesh-mountain? And yet once—it doesn't seem possible—in the scrubby bushes on Hymettos, when I was a dolt of eighteen, she said, "*Ela pethí mou*," and pulled my hand between her legs.

Sometimes I wonder what Adoni thinks of women. I swear, at twenty-five he'd never touched one. I used to say to him, every other night, "You take the evening off, Adoni, Anna and I can manage," so as to give him the opportunity; but he'd shrug, shake his head and carry on skewering kebabs. Then we started to hire waitresses. It's a good idea, if you can afford it, to hire pretty waitresses. It attracts customers, apart from easing the load. But my real reason for hiring waitresses was to encourage Adoni. I'm an immoral old man. First there was Carol, then Diane, then Christine, but Christine was the best. After we closed at night I used to get Anna to go to bed early. I'd go with her, and leave Adoni and the waitress to clear up. I'd lie in bed with one ear cocked, thinking: "It's all right, Adoni, don't have any qualms. Take your chance. Live up to your name. Don't you want that little Christine? Doesn't she make your blood hot? Take her up to your room and screw her for your Mama's and Father's sake—we won't mind." But nothing ever happened. And to make matters worse, I couldn't resist, after a time, clapping my hand, more than once, on that Christine's bottom, and poking my finger down the front of her blouse. And though no one else ever knew about it, she gave her notice, and the next waitress we got—perhaps it was just as well—was a mousy thing with a perpetual sniff.

Adoni approached his thirtieth birthday. I began to be ashamed of him. This son of mine—he wasn't a man, he wasn't a Greek; he wasn't anything. But there I go again: "this son of mine." What right did I have to that sort of shame? What right did I have to the fatherly luxury of wanting my own son to have a little more pleasure in his youth than I'd had in those miserable, famished years in Athens? The truth is I wanted a real son, the son I'd been tricked out of, not this wooden substitute. But Anna was menopausal. I was menopausal too. Sometimes I wept.

And then I began to think: It's a punishment. It's because we never told Adoni in the first place. If we'd told him, perhaps he'd have developed in a normal way, because at least he'd have known who he was. But there's no hiding a fraud when it's a matter of blood. I started to think: Perhaps he knows, perhaps he's worked it out by some sort of sixth sense and it's *he* who's punishing us. Because we're not a true mother and father to him, he's behaving as if he's nothing to us. I said to myself: Any moment he's going to come out with it: "Anna, Kosta, I can't call you Mother and Father any more." And how could I have forestalled him? By saying to him, "Adoni, you're thirty-three now—it's time you were told something"? I began to look for signs of suspicion, of rebellion in him. He only had to show the slightest coolness to Anna—if he was slow to answer her when she spoke, for example—and I'd fly into a towering rage.

Ach! Did I say I was menopausal? Did I say I was paranoid?

And then—what happens? Adoni asks for time off. He starts to go out at night, and in the afternoons too. "Of course," I say. "Take a whole day off—have a good time." And I start to breathe more easily. I don't say anything more, but I look for signs. Is he using a lot of after-shave? Is he slicking his hair? Is he trying to lose some of that premature fat and learn some modern dance steps? And I think: When the moment is ripe I'll say to him, Here, come and sit down with me, have a brandy. Now tell me, who is this nightingale? But I don't smell any after-shave; and though Adoni goes out at night he doesn't come home late; there are no stars in his eyes; and I see him, sometimes, reading these big books, the kind you blow the dust off.

"Adonaki," I say, "what do you do when you go out?"

"I go to the library."

"What the hell do you go to the library for?"

"To read books, Baba."

"But you come in at ten and eleven. The libraries don't stay open till then."

He lowers his eyes, and I smile. "Come on, *Adoni mou*, you can tell me."

And I'm surprised by what he says.

"I go to the *Neo Elleniko*, Baba."

I've heard of the *Neo Elleniko*. It is a club in Camden for so-called expatriate Greeks. It is full of old men who tell tall, repetitious stories and like to believe they are melancholy, worldly-wise exiles. They are all *trellí*. What is more, two thirds of them aren't Greeks at all. They are crazy Cypriots. I've no time for the *Neo Elleniko*.

"What do you want with all those old madmen?"

"I talk to them, Baba. I ask them questions."

Now it's my turn to drop my eyes. So Adoni really is playing the detective. He wants to have answers. Is there a gleam in his eye? Maybe some of those old fogies at the *Neo Elleniko* were around in our neighbourhood in Nea Ionia during the war, or maybe they know people who were. He's trying to get at the truth.

"They won't tell you anything but *vlakíes*." Spittle comes to my lips.

"Why are you angry, Baba?"

"I'm not angry. Don't call me 'Baba.' You're not a kid."

He shrugs. And suddenly his round, waxy, somehow far-off face seems the face of just another man, a man who could be my age—someone you meet over some minor transaction, shake hands with, then forget.

"All right. If you like the company of old men—if there aren't any better things to do—you go to the *Neo Elleniko*. Don't ask me to come too."

This was in the spring. I tell myself: It's only a matter of time. I feel like a guilty criminal. What are we going to tell all those people we've told Adoni is our son? Anna says, "Don't worry, *glikó mou*. Nothing will happen. It's all in the past. It's too late for anything to change."

And then, some time in July, he says: "Father, I want to take a holiday this summer. You don't mind? All these years I haven't taken a holiday."

I look in his eyes for any extra meaning.

"Okay—if you want to take a holiday, take a holiday. Where are you going?" But I know the answer to this one.

"I want to go to Greece, Baba."

And so he buys his air tickets and a suitcase and lightweight clothes. He can afford all this, with all the money he hasn't spent on women. And what can I do to stop him? I even envy him—stepping off the plane at Glyfada into that syrupy heat.

His holiday is fixed for a fortnight in September. I become resigned. Let him go. He's thirty-five. It's fated. Like King Oedipus he's got to ask these fool questions. He's got to find out where he came from.

And Anna says: "Why do you look so miserable, Kostaki? Our little Adoni—so serious, so *sovaró*—he's going to take a holiday. He wants a little sunshine."

The alarm goes. Anna is already up, buttoning her dress. I haven't slept a wink. I raise myself and scratch my belly. Soon, we shall have to go through it all again, the old nightly ritual. Anna's fat hands will garnish salads. Adoni will lollop round the tables. And I will have to pretend once again I'm Zorba the Greek.

Outside it's raining. Anna hoists up her sleeves like a workman.

In England now it's already autumn. But in Athens the nights are still like ovens and the pavements smell like hot biscuits.

So I get up at four to meet him at the airport, my heart beating, like a man in a cell awaiting his trial. I see him come out of Customs, and I can tell at once—there's something about the way he walks—that he knows. I can't kid myself any more he's a son of mine. But I hug him and clap him on the shoulder just like a father should, and I think of all those scenes in which fathers meet sons who have been away a long time, in far-off lands, at sea, at war, and I don't look straight at Adoni in case he sees the wet glint in my eyes.

"Eh, Adonaki—you look well. Did you have a good time? Tell me what's it like. Did you go to Vouliagmeni? Sounio? Did you get the boat to Idra? Eh, tell me, *Adoni mou*, the Athenian girls, are they still—" I raise my hand, fingers and thumb together "—*phrouta*?"

"My suitcase, Baba—" he blinks as if he never meant to say that word, and he slips free of me to go to the luggage escalator.

In the car I'm waiting for him to spit it out. I can see it's there nudging at his lips. Okay, so you've been nosing around in Nea Ionia, you've been asking questions. You haven't been on holiday at all. Say it. Get it over with, for God's sake. But he doesn't say it. Maybe he's scared, too, to speak. Instead, he tells me about Athens. There are these tourists everywhere, and nowhere to get a decent meal in the centre of town. Vouliagmeni? Yes. It crawls with close-packed bodies and you have to pay to get on a clean piece of beach. Idra? It's full of Germans, clicking their cameras.

And I realise the delapidated but companionable Greece I knew—and which Adoni knew, via my memory—isn't there any more.

"And the girls, Adonaki?"

Later that same day he gets back into his waiter's outfit, starts slicing the bread and pulling the corks, just as if he'd never been away. I'm still waiting for him to pluck up the courage. We keep eyeing each other as we pass each other with plates, and Anna looks at me anxiously in the kitchen.

But it's not until we've closed for the night that the moment comes. For I wasn't mistaken: I knew it had to come. We're sitting in the empty restaurant, sipping coffee, asking Adoni about Athens. And suddenly something Adoni says sets Anna going. Her eyes glaze. She starts remembering Nea Ionia before the war: the old balconied houses, the families along her street, the Vassilious, the Kostopoulous, the one-eyed fig-seller, Triandaphilos. I look at her ferociously. She must know this is like a cue. But perhaps she means it as a cue.

"*As to! Koutamares!* Go and make some more coffee!"

Anna shuffles off, and I know the time has come—and I know Anna will be waiting, ears pricked as she stands by the stove, until it's passed.

He lights a cigarette.

"Do you know?—I went to see if I could find Kassaveti Street. It's still there, though all the building's new. And—do you know?—I even found one of the Vassilious—Kitsos Vassiliou, he'd be a little older than me. And he told me where I could find old Elias Tsobanidis. Do you remember him?"

Yes, I remember. He seemed about seventy when I was only a boy. I'm staggered he's still alive.

He toys with his coffee cup. There's a silence like a huge weight tilting.

"You know what I am going to say, don't you?" Suddenly his face seems no longer puddingy and soft but made of something like stone.

"Yes, yes. Say it. Say it! Say it!"

"Elias Tsobanidis told me—or he said things so that I could work it out—that my real name isn't Alexopoulos—it's Melianos. My mother died when I was born and my father died in the war."

"It's true, it's true. It's the truth!" I wish I could blubber like a sinful old man.

"Forgive me, Adonaki."

But he looks at me with that hard, determined face—where has he acquired that from? He draws on his cigarette. His big fingers are leathery and blunt. And suddenly it seems not just that he's a grown man but that he's old, he's lost the youth he never had.

He puts down his cigarette, leans forward across the table, and then he says, cool as ice:

"Elias told me something else too. You know that what Elias says must be the truth, don't you? He said your name is not Alexopoulos either. The Alexopouloses were neighbours of your parents in Smyrna—they were in the tobacco business—and they were the ones who got you onto the refugee ship. Your mother and father were killed when the Turks burnt the city."

I look at him as if he is a ghost. I notice that Anna is standing in the doorway. She too looks like a ghost and she is looking at me as if I am a ghost.

We're all ghosts. But at the same time I know, I see it as plain as anything—we're all going to carry on just as before, performing our rituals in the restaurant as if nothing has changed, pretending we're people we're not.

"Elias Tsobanidis is an old liar!" I start to yell, to this "son" I've lied to all my life. "An old liar! An old liar!"

Tell me, who are we? What's important, what isn't? Is it better to live in ignorance? All my life I've felt guilty because I chopped off my mother's fingers, and now I learn it wasn't my mother at all. *Ach!* And two of those heads the Turks lopped off in Smyrna, two of them belonged to my father and mother.

Aiee! I don't like the way the world's going.

CHEMISTRY

THE POND IN OUR PARK was circular, exposed, perhaps fifty yards across. When the wind blew, little waves travelled across it and slapped the paved edges, like a miniature sea. We would go there, Mother, Grandfather and I, to sail the motor-launch Grandfather and I made out of plywood, balsawood and varnished paper. We would go even in the winter—especially in the winter, because then we would have the pond to ourselves—when the leaves on the two willows turned yellow and dropped and the water froze your hands. Mother would sit on a wooden bench set back from the perimeter; I would prepare the boat for launching. Grandfather, in his black coat and gray scarf, would walk to the far side to receive it. For some reason it was always Grandfather, never I, who went to the far side. When he reached his station I would hear his "Ready!" across the water. A puff of vapor would rise from his lips like the smoke from a muffled pistol. And I would release the launch. It worked by a battery. Its progress was laboured but its course steady. I would watch it head out to the middle while Mother watched behind me. As it moved it seemed that it followed an actual existing line between Grandfather, myself and Mother, as if Grandfather were pulling us towards him on some invisible cord, and that he had to do this to prove we were not beyond his reach. When the boat drew near him he would crouch on his haunches. His hands—which I knew were knotted, veiny and mottled from an accident in one of his chemical experiments—would reach out, grasp it and set it on its return.

The voyages were trouble-free. Grandfather improvised a wire grapnel on the end of a length of fishing line in case of shipwrecks or engine failure, but it was never used. Then one day—it must have been soon after Mother met Ralph—we watched the boat, on its first trip across the pond to Grandfather, suddenly become deeper, and deeper in the water. The motor cut. The launch wallowed, sank. Grandfather made several throws with his grapnel and pulled out clumps of green slime. I remember what he said to me, on this, the first loss in my life that I had witnessed. He said, very gravely: "You must accept it—you can't get it back—it's the only way," as if he were repeating something to himself. And I remember Mother's face as she got up from the bench to leave. It was very still and very white, as if she had seen something appalling.

It was some months after that that Ralph, who was now a regular guest at weekends, shouted over the table to Grandfather: "Why don't you leave her alone?!"

I remember it because that same Saturday Grandfather recalled the wreck of my boat, and Ralph said to me, as if pouncing on something: "How about me buying you a new one? How would you like that?" And I said, just to see his face go crestfallen and blank, "No!" several times, fiercely. Then as we ate supper Ralph suddenly barked, as Grandfather was talking to Mother: "Why don't you leave her alone?!"

Grandfather looked at him. "Leave her alone? What do you know about being left alone?" Then he glanced from Ralph to Mother. And Ralph didn't answer, but his face went tight and his hands clenched on his knife and fork.

And all this was because Grandfather had said to Mother: "You don't make curry any more, the way you did for Alex, the way Vera taught you."

It was Grandfather's house we lived in—with Ralph as an ever more permanent lodger. Grandfather and Grandmother had lived in it almost since the day of their marriage. My grandfather had worked for a firm which manufactured gold- and silver-plated articles. My grandmother died suddenly when I was only four; and all I know is that I must have had her looks. My mother said so and so did my father; and Grandfather, without saying anything, would often gaze curiously into my face.

At that time Mother, Father and I lived in a new house some distance from Grandfather's. Grandfather took his wife's death very badly. He needed the company of his daughter and my father; but he refused to leave the house in which my grandmother had lived, and my parents refused to leave theirs. There was bitterness all around, which I scarcely appreciated. Grandfather remained alone in his house, which he ceased to maintain, spending more and more time in his garden shed which he had fitted out for his hobbies of model making and amateur chemistry.

The situation was resolved in a dreadful way: by my own father's death.

He was required now and then to fly to Dublin or Cork in the light aeroplane belonging to the company he worked for, which imported Irish goods. One day, in unexceptional weather conditions, the aircraft disappeared without trace into the Irish Sea. In a state which resembled a kind of trance—as if some outside force were all the time directing her—my Mother sold up our house, put away the money for our joint future, and moved in with Grandfather.

My father's death was a far less remote event than my grandmother's, but no more explicable. I was only seven. Mother said, amidst her adult grief: "He has gone to where Grandma's gone." I wondered how Grandmother could be at the bottom of the Irish Sea, and at the same time what Father was doing there. I wanted to know when he would return. Perhaps I knew, even as I asked this, that he never would, that my childish assumptions were only a way of allaying my own grief. But if I really believed Father was gone forever—I was wrong.

Perhaps too I was endowed with my father's looks no less than my grandmother's. Because when my mother looked at me she would often break into uncontrollable tears and she would clasp me for long periods without letting go, as if afraid I might turn to air.

I don't know if Grandfather took a secret, vengeful delight in my father's death, or if he was capable of it. But fate had made him and his daughter quits and reconciled them in mutual grief. Their situations were equivalent: she a widow and he a widower. And just as my mother could see in me a vestige of my father, so Grandfather could see in the two of us a vestige of my grandmother.

For about a year we lived quietly, calmly, even contentedly within the scope of this sad symmetry. We scarcely made any contact with the outside world. Grandfather still worked, though his retirement age had passed, and would not let Mother work. He kept Mother and me as he might have kept his own wife and son. Even when he did retire we lived quite comfortably on his pension, some savings and a widow's pension my mother got. Grandfather's health showed signs of weakening—he became rheumatic and sometimes short of breath—but he would still go out to the shed in the garden to conduct his chemical experiments, over which he hummed and chuckled gratefully to himself.

We forgot we were three generations. Grandfather bought Mother bracelets and ear-rings. Mother called me her "little man." We lived for each other—and for those two unfaded memories—and for a whole year, a whole harmonious year, we were really quite happy. Until that day in the park when my boat, setting out across the pond toward Grandfather, sank.

Sometimes when Grandfather provoked Ralph I thought Ralph would be quite capable of jumping to his feet, reaching across the table, seizing Grandfather by the throat and choking him. He was a big man, who ate heartily, and I was often afraid he might hit me. But Mother somehow kept him in check. Since Ralph's appearance she had grown neglectful of Grandfather. For example—as Grandfather had pointed out that evening—she would cook the things that Ralph liked (rich, thick stews, but not curry) and forget to produce the meals that Grandfather was fond of. But no matter how neglectful and even hurtful she might be to Grandfather herself, she wouldn't have forgiven someone else's hurting him. It would have been the end of her and Ralph. And no matter how much she might hurt Grandfather—to show her allegiance to Ralph—the truth was she really did want to stick by him. She still needed—she couldn't break free of it—that delicate equilibrium that she, he and I had constructed over the months.

I suppose the question was how far Ralph could tolerate not letting go with Grandfather so as to keep Mother, or how far Mother was prepared to turn against Grandfather so as not to lose Ralph. I remember keeping a sort of equation in my head: If Ralph hurts Grandfather it means I'm right—he doesn't really care about Mother at all; not if Mother is cruel to Grandfather (though she would only be cruel to him because she couldn't forsake him) it means she really loves Ralph.

• • •

But Ralph only went pale and rigid and stared at Grandfather without moving.

Grandfather picked at his stew. We had already finished ours. He deliberately ate slowly to provoke Ralph.

Then Ralph turned to Mother and said: "For Christ's sake we're not waiting all night for him to finish!" Mother blinked and looked frightened. "Get the pudding!"

You see, he liked his food.

Mother rose slowly and gathered our plates. She looked at me and said, "Come and help."

In the kitchen she put down the plates and leaned for several seconds, her back towards me, against the draining board. Then she turned. "What am I going to do?" She gripped my shoulders. I remembered these were just the words she'd used once before, very soon after father's death, and then, too, her face had had the same quivery look of being about to spill over. She pulled me towards her. I had a feeling of being back in that old impregnable domain which Ralph had not yet penetrated. Through the window, half visible in the twilight, the evergreen shrubs which filled our garden were defying the onset of autumn. Only the cherry laurel bushes were partly denuded—for some reason Grandfather had been picking their leaves. I didn't know what to do or say—I should have said something—but inside I was starting to form a plan.

Mother took her hands from me and straightened up. Her face was composed again. She took the apple-crumble from the oven. Burnt sugar and apple juice seethed for a moment on the edge of the dish. She handed me the bowl of custard. We strode, resolutely, back to the table. I thought: Now we are going to face Ralph, now we are going to show our solidarity. Then she put down the crumble, began spooning out helpings and said to Grandfather, who was still tackling his stew: "You're ruining our meal—do you want to take yours out to your shed?!"

• • •

Grandfather's shed was more than just a shed. Built of brick in one corner of the high walls surrounding the garden, it was large enough to accommodate a stove, a sink, an old armchair, as well as Grandfather's work-benches and apparatus, and to serve—as it was serving Grandfather more and more—as a miniature home.

I was always wary of entering it. It seemed to me, even before Ralph, even when Grandfather and I constructed the model launch, that it was somewhere where Grandfather went to be alone, undisturbed, to commune perhaps, in some obscure way, with my dead grandmother. But that evening I did not hesitate. I walked along the path by the ivy-clad garden wall. It seemed that his invitation, his loneliness were written in a form only I could read on the dark green door. And when I opened it he said: "I thought you would come."

I don't think Grandfather practised chemistry for any particular reason. He studied it from curiosity and for solace, as some people study the structure of cells under a microscope or watch the changing formation of clouds. In those weeks after Mother drove him out I learnt from Grandfather the fundamentals of chemistry.

I felt safe in his shed. The house where Ralph now lorded it, tucking into bigger and bigger meals, was a menacing place. The shed was another, a sealed-off world. It had a salty, mineral, unhuman smell. Grandfather's flasks, tubes and retort stands would be spread over his work-bench. His chemicals were acquired through connections in the metal-plating trade. The stove would be lit in the corner. Beside it would be his meal tray—for, to shame Mother, Grandfather had taken to eating his meals regularly in the shed. A single electric light bulb hung from a beam in the roof. A gas cylinder fed his burners. On one wall was a glass fronted cupboard in which he grew alum and copper sulphate crystals.

I would watch Grandfather's experiments. I would ask him to explain what he was doing and to name the contents of his various bottles.

And Grandfather wasn't the same person in his shed as he was in the house—sour and cantankerous. He was a weary, ailing man who winced now and then because of his rheumatism and spoke with quiet self-absorption.

"What are you making, Grandpa?"

"Not making—changing. Chemistry is the science of change. You don't make things in chemistry—you change them. Anything can change."

He demonstrated the point by dissolving marble chips in nitric acid. I watched fascinated.

But he went on: "Anything can change. Even gold can change."

He poured a little of the nitric acid into a beaker, then took another jar of colourless liquid and added some of its contents to the nitric acid. He stirred the mixture with a glass rod and heated it gently. Some brown fumes came off.

"Hydrochloric acid and nitric acid. Neither would work by itself, but the mixture will."

Lying on the bench was a pocket watch with a gold chain. I knew it had been given to Grandfather long ago by my grandmother. He unclipped the chain from the watch, then, leaning forward against the bench, he held it between two fingers over the beaker. The chain swung. He eyed me as if he were waiting for me to give some sign. Then he drew the chain away from the beaker.

"You'll have to take my word for it, eh?"

He picked up the watch and reattached it to the chain.

"My old job—gold-plating. We used to take real gold and change it. Then we'd take something that wasn't gold at all and cover it with this changed gold so it looked as if it was all gold—but it wasn't."

He smiled bitterly.

"What are we going to do?"

"Grandpa?"

"People change too, don't they?"

He came close to me. I was barely ten. I looked at him without speaking.

"Don't they?"

He stared fixedly into my eyes, the way I remembered him doing after Grandmother's death.

"They change. But the elements don't change. Do you know what an element is? Gold's an element. We turned it from one form into another, but we didn't make any gold—or lose any."

Then I had a strange sensation. It seemed to me that Grandfather's face before me was only a cross section from some infinite stick of rock, from which, at the right point, Mother's face and mine might also be cut. I thought: Every face is like this. I had a sudden giddying feeling that there is no end to anything. I wanted to be told simple, precise facts.

"What's that, Grandpa?"

"Hydrochloric acid."

"And that?"

"Green vitriol."

"And that?" I pointed to another, unlabelled jar of clear liquid, which stood at the end of the bench, attached to a complex piece of apparatus.

"Laurel water. Prussic acid." He smiled. "Not for drinking."

All that autumn was exceptionally cold. The evenings were chill and full of rustlings of leaves. When I returned to the house from taking out Grandfather's meal tray (this had become my duty) I would observe Mother and Ralph in the living room through the open kitchen hatchway. They would drink a lot from the bottles of whisky and vodka which Ralph brought in and which at first Mother made a show of disapproving. The drink made Mother go soft and heavy and blurred and it made Ralph gain in authority. They would slump together on the sofa. One night I watched Ralph pull Mother towards him and hold her in his arms, his big lurching frame almost enveloping her, and Mother saw me, over Ralph's shoulder, watching from the hatchway. She looked trapped and helpless.

And that was the night that I got my chance—when I went to collect Grandfather's tray. When I entered the shed he was asleep in his chair, his plates, barely touched, on the tray at his feet. In his slumber—his hair disheveled, mouth open—he looked like some torpid, captive animal that has lost even the will to eat. I had taken an empty spice jar from the kitchen. I took the glass bottle labelled HNO_3 and poured some of its contents, carefully, into the spice jar. Then I picked up Grandfather's tray, placed the spice jar beside the plates and carried the tray to the house.

I thought I would throw the acid in Ralphs's face at breakfast. I didn't want to kill him. It would have been pointless to kill him—since death is a deceptive business. I wanted to spoil his face so Mother would no longer want him. I took the spice jar to my room and hid it in my bedside cupboard. In the morning I would smuggle it down in my trouser pocket. I would wait, pick my moment. Under the table I would remove the stopper. As Ralph gobbled down his eggs and fried bread...

I thought I would not be able to sleep. From my bedroom window I could see the dark square of the garden and the little patch of light cast from the window of Grandfather's shed. Often I could not sleep until I had seen that patch of light disappear and I knew that Grandfather had shuffled back to the house and slipped in, like a stray cat, at the back door.

But I must have slept that night, for I do not remember seeing Grandfather's light go out or hearing his steps on the garden path.

That night Father came into my bedroom. I knew it was him.

His hair and clothes were wet, his lips were caked with salt; seaweed hung from his shoulders. He came and stood by my bed. Where he trod, pools of water formed on the carpet and slowly oozed outwards. For a long time he looked at me. Then he said: "It was her. She made a hole in the bottom of the boat, not big enough to notice, so it would sink—so you and Grandfather would watch it sink. The boat sank—like my plane." He gestured to his dripping clothes and encrusted lips. "Don't you believe me?" He held out a hand to me but I was afraid to take it. "Don't you believe me? Don't you believe me?" And as he repeated this he walked slowly backwards towards the door, as if something were pulling him, the pools of water at his feet drying instantly. And it was only when he had disappeared that I managed to speak and said: "Yes. I believe you. I'll prove it."

And then it was almost light and rain was dashing against the window as if the house were plunging under water and a strange, small voice was calling from the front of the house—but it wasn't Father's voice. I got up, walked out onto the landing and peered through the landing window. The voice was a voice on the radio inside an ambulance which was parked with its doors open by the pavement. The heavy rain and the tossing branches of a rowan tree obscured my view, but I saw the two men in uniform carrying out the stretcher with a blanket draped over it. Ralph was with them. He was wearing his dressing gown and pyjamas and slippers over bare feet, and he carried an umbrella. He fussed around the ambulance men like an overseer directing the loading of some vital piece of cargo. He called something to Mother who must have been standing below, out of sight at the front door. I ran back across the landing. I wanted to get the acid. But then Mother came up the stairs. She was wearing her dressing gown. She caught me in her arms. I smelt whisky. She said: "Darling. Please, I'll explain. Darling, darling."

But she never did explain. All her life since then, I think, she has been trying to explain, or to avoid explaining. She only said:

"Grandpa was old and ill, he wouldn't have lived much longer anyway." And there was the official verdict: suicide by swallowing prussic acid. but all the other things that should have been explained—or confessed—she never did explain.

And she wore, beneath everything, this look of relief, as if she had recovered from an illness. Only a week after Grandfather's funeral she went into Grandfather's bedroom and flung wide the windows. It was a brilliant, crisp late-November day and the leaves on the rowan tree were all gold. And she said: "There—isn't that lovely?"

The day of Grandfather's funeral had been such a day—hard, dazzling, spangled with early frost and gold leaves. We stood at the ceremony, Mother, Ralph and I, like a mock version of the trio—Grandfather, Mother and I—who had once stood at my father's memorial service. Mother did not cry. She had not cried at all, even in the days before the funeral when the policemen and the officials from the coroner's court came, writing down their statements, apologising for their intrusion and asking their questions.

They did not address their questions to me. Mother said: "He's only ten, what can he know?" Though there were a thousand things I wanted to tell them—about how Mother banished Grandfather, about how suicide can be murder and how things don't end—which made me feel that I was somehow under suspicion. I took the jar of acid from my bedroom, went to the park and threw it in the pond.

And then after the funeral, after the policemen and officials had gone, Mother and Ralph began to clear out the house and to remove the things from the shed. They tidied the overgrown parts of the garden and clipped back the trees. Ralph wore an old sweater which was far too small for him and I recognised it as one of Father's. And Mother said: "We're going to move to a new house soon—Ralph's buying it."

I had nowhere to go. I went down to the park and stood by the pond. Dead willow leaves floated on it. Beneath its surface was a bottle of acid and the wreck of my launch. But though things change they aren't destroyed. It was there, by the pond, when dusk was gathering and it was almost time for the park gates to be locked, as I looked to the centre where my launch sank, then up again to the far side, that I saw him. He was standing in his black overcoat and his grey scarf. The air was very cold and little waves were running across the water. He was smiling, and I knew: The launch was still travelling over to him, unstoppable, unsinkable, along that invisible line. And his hands, his acid-marked hands, would reach out to receive it.

CLIFFEDGE

WHAT IS IT ABOUT THE sea that summons people to it? That beckons the idle to play and ponder at its skirts? What was it that built these ice-cream coloured colonies, these outposts of pleasure along the clifftops and shingle of the south coast? Pleasure of being on the brink? Pleasure in the precariousness of pleasure? How would they have become so strangely intense, so strangely all-in-all, these little worlds (the pier, the life-boat station, the aquarium) we once knew for two weeks out of every fifty-two, were it not for their being pressed against this sleeping monster, the sea?

We came here long ago, Neil and I. To—let me call it, for reasons of my own—Cliffedge. We arrived every August on the train with our parents. It had then the peculiar set-apart redolence of "holidays." Foreign, enchanting, but not real. It might—it ought to—have remained no more than a memory, lingering yet fading, like the fading photographs taken at the time: the two of us buried up to our necks in sand; or splashing in the waves. Neil, two years my younger, the slighter, more angular, more excitable figure.

I could not have imagined that in fifteen, in twenty years' time that world of salt and sunburn would not yet have passed into remembrance. That I would still be going with my brother, he thirty-three, I thirty-five, to the same resort; that I would buy him on the train, not lemonade and chocolate as Mother and Father did, but beer and cigarettes; that I would watch him—as if indeed I had taken over the former roles of my parents—on the clifftops, on the pebbles, playing his dangerous games.

I said to Mary: I have this brother who has never grown up. I have to take him every so often on outings and pleasure trips, even on holidays to the seaside. This is serious and necessary. What makes it serious is that unlike children when their pleasures are denied them, Neil does not merely throw tantrums. He threatens to kill himself. I was wary, apologetic. Mary frowned, looked momentarily grave, even a little aggrieved; then, putting her hand on mine, she gave her bright, slightly hard expression—an expression I have come to know so well, along with its secret meaning: I can look out for myself; there is no question of my ability. She squeezed my hand and smiled. Then she said, "I'm sure we can cope." And that word, also, I have come to know well—to regard it almost as Mary's motto and philosophy in a single sound: "Cope."

That was years ago too, before we married. And Mary could not perhaps have known how deadly earnest I had been in my warnings. How what at first had seemed a trying if manageable obstacle, to be surmounted in time, became an irremovable burden. How her "coping" (for she never failed to cope) was to progress first to a kind of righteous detachment—It is *your* problem, I do not deserve to be impeded by it—then to the pitch where, when I would take Neil on his "holidays," she too would take holidays of her own (it was unthinkable that the three of us could have gone away together); holidays which I was not slow to understand were spent in the company of her lover.

I remember one summer long ago at Cliffedge Neil wanted to take a trip on one of the boats the fishermen used for taking parties mackerel fishing. The weather was unfavourable—the sky overcast, the sea heaving sluggishly—but it was the last day of our holiday and my father (who, so I know now, had his own cause for reluctance) yielded. We set off. Beyond the shelter of the bay the swell became suddenly heavy, a squally wind slapped us. I became seasick. My father was grimly silent. Neil did not have the least qualm. He caught six mackerel that day, hauling them in on the end of the line the fisherman prepared. He leant well out of the boat, eyes on the taut nylon as it cut the water. As the boat began to pitch and roll his face became flushed with ferocious glee. I had this sudden feeling that I must look after Neil, that I must protect him. But at the same time nausea assailed me. I spent the rest of that fishing trip fighting my stomach—fighting too what I can only describe as *fear of the waves*—and when I finally spewed up, weak-legged, over the harbour wall, it was Neil who looked at me—his six bloody-gilled mackerel looped on a string—as if I needed protection.

It required no expert in psychology to see that Neil had never broken free from childhood. At twenty he was still living in the same world he had inhabited at eight, still pursuing, in some obstinate inner space, the same infant quests he had pursued at Cliffedge. It was when he was sixteen (the year after Mother and Father died and his last at school—the teachers noticed the distressing signs) that he made his first attempts on his life. That year, too, began his innumerable spells as a hospital inmate—and my dutiful, wearisome visits. The doctors achieved little.

Whenever he was discharged they would advise, in their half-hearted way, a period of rest, a change of air. I would say, But he only wants to be taken to Cliffedge. Wouldn't that exacerbate, entrench the problem? Yes, they would say, with a shrug, but sometimes there were risks too on the other side—in not letting the patient have his way.

And so we came to Cliffedge. Year after year. And I would be half this genial and obliging uncle (Take me on the toy railway. Please. Take me on the crazy golf) and half this solemn warden (A boat trip? No, no boat trips. A walk on the cliff? Only if you promise—*promise*—to keep to the path). I dared not let him out of my sight. At night, in our hotel room, after I had put him, drugged, to bed, like a tired child, I used to long to slip out to one of the bars by the seafront and talk to some ordinary man—a salesman or gas fitter on holiday with his family. I would think: If Neil were not the way he was, if he were just my brother, we would stand each other drinks, talk about our jobs, our wives. I would lie awake, listening to him muttering in his strange, busy dreams, and say to myself: My God, what he owes to me, how much he owes to me. The hotel plumbing would gurgle and it would seem to me that I was chained and anchored to this hotel bedroom, to this seaside resort which I had known as a boy. As if my life were really only a small, contracted thing which had never passed certain limits. And then I would think of Mary.

When I was seventeen my father confided in me his fear of water. He was a strong, dependable man, not given to talking about himself. I took this disclosure as a sign of trust and initiation, as a sign of my own coming of age; and yet I remember I also despised him for his admission and I experienced a pang of disappointment—as I recall it now, I experience it again—that this solid, self-contained man whom I emulated was the victim of such an irrational weakness. He could not swim and he had always been uneasy (he alluded to that boat trip of several years before) at any journey on water. It was absurd, but he would rather travel for miles over land than make a simple sea crossing. All of which was cruelly ironic; for less than six months later—I was suddenly the head of a family of two—he and Mother were to die in a motor accident.

There are couples who marry out of feeling and there are couples who marry precisely in order to conceal their feelings. Mary and I have always been of this second category. It is as though we reached an understanding at the beginning that what affected us inwardly was our own and strictly private affair, an encumbrance not to be imposed on the other, and that our relationship was to be one of practical workability. Mary had a lightness, a lack of anything intense, which used to tantalise me. But what impressed me most about her in those early days was her aura of competence and decision, her air of offering me a partnership in an efficient, grown-up progress through the world. Whenever we discussed Neil, it was to speak of him as a nuisance, an inconvenience, who was nonetheless not to be allowed to upset the smooth business-like machinery of our marriage. And I was glad of this brisk attitude which seemed to clear so much space.

And yet Neil became, over the years, less the nuisance, more a necessity. He gave Mary cause for a constant entitlement to compensation, and placed on me the constant onus of redress. My relations with my brother were to be kept apart but, in so far as they impinged on Mary, she was to be allowed in return her own separate concessions. It was during perhaps the fifth year of our marriage that I first understood she had a lover. This was not a circumstance, either, to interfere with our marital efficiency. We remained the capable, well-matched couple whom our friends, I genuinely believe, respected and admired. Our task became to demonstrate that such we were. And yet it seems to me now that this profession of strength depended all along on

Neil. Neil was the unmentioned foil to our competence, the gauge of our stability. Was it possible that Mary had married me, in some obscure, paradoxical way, because of Neil?

I did my best to find out about her lover. By the tacit rules we had imposed on ourselves this was forbidden—but I discovered nothing, not even his name. Mary was scrupulous in the conduct of her affair and, short of hiring a private detective, I could ascertain little. She was fully aware that I had my suspicions, but her attitude to this might have been expressed, had it ever been uttered, in the word, "Very well, you know what I am doing. But then—you are perfectly free to do the same." To which she might have added the rider: "Though you would not be able to exercise the same control, would you?" And, indeed, one of the notable things about Mary's "holidays" is the way they were kept within strict and defined limits. Returning from them, she would slip calmly back into the routines of our marriage without any spilling over from the one compartment into the other. She has this talent for organising and administering to her needs, as if she were measuring out slightly bad-tasting but beneficial medicines. Thus it seems to me that she always rationed meticulously the sexual element in our marriage, as if aware of some danger amidst the pleasure.

One evening when I visited Neil in his hospital something suddenly became clear to me. Over the years, I had come to regard Neil less and less as my brother. When I visited him or took him on those trips to Cliffedge he became, increasingly, simply a charge, a liability. I was doing my duty, like a father towards a bastard child. In a strange way Neil had ceased even to resemble me physically. His appearance—it is hard to know how to put this—had taken on, after all those spells of "treatment," a roughness, a wildness, as if he had just returned from an arduous trip to some forsaken part of the earth. He was scarcely civilised; and yet beneath it all, if you looked, was the delicacy and simplicity of a child. Sometimes when I arrived at the hospital he would blink warningly at me, as if I were trespassing, presuming. What overcame me that evening was not just the thought, which now and then would pierce me, that this alien creature was my brother, but the fact that I envied him.

When I returned that night to Mary she was sitting, smoking a cigarette, with the air she adopts on such and other occasions of a woman kept waiting for an appointment. I knew at once, by the look both of alertness and of slight distaste in her face that she detected a change of mood in me. I did not sit down. I wanted to see her moved, just for once, by anger, fear. She drew on her cigarette and, as was her usual practice, declined to ask about Neil. Her cool, cosmetic poise suddenly repelled me. It struck me that possibly I had been wrong about the even, mutual arrangement of our marriage. That all along Mary had regarded me, in some measure, as I regarded Neil; that she was observing me, testing me by her, not our, rules of maturity. Perhaps she was waiting for me, even then—half daring me—to defy the rules, to relax my guard. And what would happen if I did? Perhaps she would go to live permanently with her lover.

"Why don't you ask about Neil?!" I screamed in her face. "Ask about Neil, you bitch!"

There was no need for either of us to seek reasons for this crude—and ineffective—outburst. I picked up an ash-tray. A glass ashtray. I wanted to throw it at her. But she said quietly: "Don't be foolish. Don't be a child."

The white cliffs rear up on either inside of Cliffedge like watchful giants. Neil always loved to walk on the cliffs. Even on those early holidays he was always wandering from the safe sand to those extremities of the beach where the chalk towered and boulders strewed the water's edge. Once he said, pointing to a less precipitous section where a sort of gully had been worn out, "There's a path, let's climb up." But I have never seen the point of purposeless risks, of courting disaster. No, I said, as if to warn him.

And that last time, that last walk on the cliffs (past the coastguard station, the plinth commemorating some nineteenth century wreck) I was as vigilant as ever, as dutiful as ever. No, Neil—away from the edge. But perhaps for one moment I relaxed my guard, perhaps I was thinking of other things: of Mary between the sheets with her medicinal lover; or perhaps I was looking down at the distant ribbon of the town, at the scraps of colour still littering the evening beach, at the sunlight catching the pier pavilion and the seafront hotels, and was thinking: It will only add spice to their holiday gaiety, it will only send a thrill through the sprawling crowds on the beach to learn of it. "Death Plunge," Brothers in Seaside Tragedy." Perhaps I shouldn't have said to him, "Don't you know how much you owe to me? *Don't you?*"

Mary left a month ago. I have brought too many forbidden things into her life and so broken our contract. But I know now that she has not left me out of contempt, out of cold-blooded rejection, but out of fear. She was frightened. Those first days after Neil's death I cried like a baby. I had never cried in front of Mary before. And through my tears I saw in her face something more than intolerance or disgust—I saw horror.

But the inquest cleared me of suspicion. They declared an open verdict. They recognised that Neil was not an ordinary case, and that I had been like a father to him. I am free now. Free of a wife, and free, some would say, of a burdensome brother. But if I wished to be free of him, if I wished to be done with those repeated obligations, those repeated scenes he imposed on my life, why should I have returned, these last three weekends, to Cliffedge? To the same hotel, the same seafront, the same miniature but—as I know it now—far from simple world that has shadowed me from childhood?

I have been looking for Neil. That is why. I do not believe he is dead. He cannot have deserted me. Some day, by one of the familiar spots—the band-stand, the Harbour Café, the putting green—I will find him. He will be just one of the many "lost children" of the beach.

At night I do not seek ordinary company in pubs. I lie awake in the hotel room hoping to hear Neil murmur in his sleep. I feel so afraid. The gurgling of the pipes turns into the roar of great oceans. When I sleep I have this dream. I am alone in the boat. I am leaning over the side looking at my line disappearing into the water. I know that Neil is somewhere there in the depths and I will catch him. I start to pull in. A storm is brewing and the waves are rising up against the boat. I pull and pull so as to catch him in time. But the line is endless.

THE WATCH

*

TELL ME, WHAT IS MORE magical, more sinister, more malign yet consoling, more expressive of the constancy—and fickleness—of fate than a clock? Think of the clock which is ticking now, behind you, above you, peeping from your cuff. Think of the watches which chirp blithely on the wrists of the newly dead. Think of those clocks which are prayed to so that their hands might never register some moment of doom—but they jerk forward nonetheless; or, conversely, of those clocks which are begged to hasten their movement so that some span of misery might reach its end, but they stubbornly refuse to budge. Think of those clocks, gently chiming on mantelpieces, which soothe one man and attack the nerves of another. And think of that clock, renowned in song, which when its old master died, stopped also, like a faithfull mastiff, never to go again. Is it so remarkable to imagine—as savages once did on first seeing them—that in these whirring, clicking mechanisms there lives a spirit, a power, a demon?

My family is—was—a family of clockmakers. Three generations ago, driven by political turmoils, they fled to England from the Polish city of Lublin, a city famous for its baroque buildings, for its cunning artifacts—for clocks. For two centuries the Krepskis fashioned the clocks of Lublin. But Krepski, it is claimed, is only a corruption of the German Krepf, and, trace back further my family line and you will find connections with the great horologers of Nuremberg and Prague. For my forefathers were no mere craftsmen, no mere technicians. Pale, myopic men they may have been, sitting in dim workshops, counting the money they made by keeping the local gentry punctual; but they were also sorcerers, men of mission. They shared a primitive but unshakeable faith that clocks and watches not only recorded time, but contained it—they spun it with their loom-like motion. That clocks, indeed, were the *cause* of time. That without their assiduous tick-tocking, present and future would never meet, oblivion would reign, and the world would vanish down its own gullet in some self-annihilating instant.

The man who regards his watch every so often, who thinks of time as something fixed and arranged, like a calendar, and not as a power to which is owed the very beating of his heart, may easily scoff. My family's faith is not to be communicated by appeals to reason. And yet in our case there is one unique and clinching item of evidence, one undeniable and sacred repository of material proof.

No one can say why, of all my worthy ancestors, my great-grandfather Stanislaw should have been singled out. No one can determine what mysterious conjunction of influences, what gatherings of instinct, knowledge and skill made the moment propitious. But on a September day, in Lublin, in 1809, my great-grandfather made the breakthrough which to the clockmaker is as the elixir to the alchemist. He created a clock which would not only function perpetually without winding, but from which time itself, that invisible yet palpable essence, could actually be gleaned—by contact, by proximity—like some form of magnetic charge. So, at least, it proved. The properties of this clock—or large pocket-watch, to be precise, for its benefits necessitated that it be easily carried—were not immediately observable. My great-grandfather had only an uncanny intuition. In his diary for that September day he writes cryptically: "The new watch—I know, feel it in my blood—it is the *one*." Thereafter, at weekly intervals, the same entry: "The new watch—not yet wound." The weekly interval lapses into a monthly one. Then, on September 3rd, 1810—the exact anniversary of the watch's birth—the entry: "The Watch—a whole year without winding," to which is added the mystical statement: "We shall live for ever."

But this was not all. I write now in the 1970s. In 1809 my great-grandfather was forty-two. Simple arithmetic will indicate that we are dealing here with extraordinary longevity. My great-grandfather died in 1900—a man of one hundred and thirty-three, by this time an established and industrious clockmaker in one of the immigrant quarters of London. He was then, as a faded daguerrotype testifies, a man certainly old in appearance but not decrepit (you would have judged him perhaps a hale seventy), still on his feet and still busy at his trade; and he died not from senility but from being struck by an ill-managed horse-drawn omnibus while attempting one July day to cross Ludgate Hill. From this it will be seen that my great-grandfather's watch did not confer immortality. It gave to those who had access to it a perhaps indefinite store of years; it was proof against age and against all those processes by which we are able to say that a man's time runs out, but it was not proof against external accident. Witness the death of Juliusz, my great-grandfather's first-born, killed by a Russian musket-ball in 1807. And Josef, the second-born, who came to a violent end in the troubles which forced my great-grandfather to flee his country.

To come closer home. In 1900 my grandfather, Feliks (my great-grandfather's third son), was a mere stripling of ninety-two. Born in 1808, and therefore receiving almost immediate benefit from my great-grandfather's watch, he was even sounder in limb, relatively speaking, than his father. I can vouch for this because (though, in 1900, I was yet to be conceived) I am now speaking of a man whom I have known intimately for the greater part of my own life and who, indeed, reared me almost from birth.

In every respect my grandfather was the disciple and image of my great-grandfather. He worked long and hard at the workshop in East London where he and Stanislaw, though blessed among mortals, still laboured at the daily business of our family. As he grew older—and still older—he acquired the solemn, vigilant and somewhat miserly looks of my great-grandfather. In 1900 he was the only remaining son and heir—for Stanislaw, by wondrous self-discipline, considering his length of years, had refrained from begetting further children, having foreseen the jealousies and divisions that the watch might arouse in a large family.

Feliks thus became the guardian of the watch which had now ticked away unwound for little short of a century. Its power was undiminished. Feliks lived on to the age of one hundred and sixty-one. He met his death, in brazen and spectacular fashion, but a few years ago, from a bolt of lightning, whilst walking in a violent storm in the Sussex downs. I myself can bear witness to his vigour, both of body and mind, at that more-than-ripe old age. For I myself watched him tramp off defiantly on that August night. I myself pleaded with him to heed the fury of the weather. And, after he failed to return, it was I who discovered his rain-soaked body, at the foot of a split tree, and pulled from his waistcoat pocket, on the end of its gold chain, the Great Watch—still ticking.

• • •

But what of my father? Where was he while my grandfather took me in charge? That is another story—which we shall come to shortly. One of perversity and rebellion, and one, so my grandfather was never slow to remind me, which cast a shadow on our family honour and pride.

You will note that I mave made no mention of the womenfolk of our family. Futhermore, I have said that Stanislaw took what must be considered some pains to limit his progeny. Increase in years, you might suppose, would lead to increase in issue. But this was not so—and Great-grandfather's feat was, perhaps, not so formidable. Consider the position of a man who has the prospect before him of extraordinary length of years and who looks back at his own past as other men look at history books. The limits of his being, his "place in time," as the phrase goes, the fact of his perishability begin to fade and he begins not to interest himself in those means by which other men seek to prolong their existence. And of these, what is more universal than the begetting of children, the passing on of one's own blood?

Because they were little moved by the breeding instinct my great-grandfather and my grandfather were little moved by women. The wives they had—both of them got through three—followed very much the Oriental pattern where women are little more than the property of their husbands. Chosen neither for their beauty nor fecundity but more for blind docility, they were kept apart from the masculine mysteries of clock-making and were only acquainted with the Great Watch on a sort of concessionary basis. If the only one of them I knew myself—my grandfather's last wife Eleanor—is anything to go by, they were slavish, silent, timid creatures, living in a kind of bemused remoteness from their husbands (who, after all, might be more than twice their age).

I remember my grandfather once expatiating on the reasons

for this subjection and exclusion of women. "Women, you see," he warned, "have no sense of time, they do not appreciate the urgency of things—that is what puts them in their place"—an explanation which I found unpersuasive then, perhaps because I was a young man and not uninterested in young women. But the years have confirmed the—painful—truth of my grandfather's judgement. Show me a woman who has the same urgency as a man. Show me a woman who cares as much about the impending deadline, the ticking seconds, the vanishing hours. Ah yes, you will say, this is masculine humbug. Ah yes, I betray all the prejudice and contempt which ruined my brief marriage—which has ruined my life. But look at the matter on a broader plane. In the natural order of things it is women who are the longer lived. Why is this? Is it not precisely because they lack urgency—that urgency which preoccupies men, which drives them to unnatural subterfuges and desperate acts, which exhausts them and ushers them to an early death?

But urgency—despite his words—was not something that showed much in my grandfather's face. Understandably. For endowed with a theoretically infinite stock of time, what cause did he have for urgency? I have spoken of my elders' miserly and watchful looks. But this miserliness was not the miserliness of restless and rapacious greed; it was the contented, vacant miserliness of the miser who sits happily on a vast hoard of money which he has no intention of spending. And the watchfulness was not a sentry-like alertness; it was more the smug superciliousness of a man who knows he occupies a unique vantage point. In fact it is true to say, the longer my forefathers lived, the less animated they became. The more they immersed themselves in their obsession with time, the more they sank in their actions into mechanical and unvarying routine, tick-tocking their lives out like the miraculous instrument that enabled them to do so.

They did not want excitement, these Methuselahs, they dreamt no dreams. Nothing characterises more my life with my grandfather than the memory of countless monotonous evenings in the house he had at Highgate—evenings in which my guardian (that man who was born before Waterloo) would sit after dinner, intent, so it would seem, on nothing other than the process of his own digestion, while my grandmother would batten herself down in some inoffensive wifely task—darning socks, sewing buttons—and the silence, the heavy, aching silence (how the memory of certain silences can weigh upon you), would be punctuated only—by the tick of clocks.

Once I dared to break this silence, to challenge this laden oppression of Time. I was a healthy, well-fed boy of thirteen. At such an age—who can deny it?—there is freshness. The moments slip by and you do not stop to count them. It was a summer evening and Highgate had, in those days, a verdant, even pastoral air. My grandfather was expounding (picture a boy of thirteen, a man of a hundred and twenty) upon his only subject when I interrupted him to ask: "But isn't it best when we forget time?"

I am sure that with these ingenuous words there rose in me—only to hold brief sway—the spirit of my rebellious, and dead, father. I was not aware of the depths of my heresy. My grandfather's face took on the look of those fathers who are in the habit of removing their belts and applying them to their sons' hides. He did not remove his belt. Instead, I received the lashings of a terrible diatribe upon the folly of a world—of which my words were a very motto—which dared to believe that Time could take care of itself; followed by an invocation of the toils of my ancestors; followed, inevitably, by a calling down upon my head of the sins of my father. As I cringed before all this I acknowledged the indissoluble, if irrational, link between age and authority. Youth must bow to age. This was the god-like fury of one hundred and twenty years beating down on me and I had no choice but to prostrate myself. And yet, simultaneously—as the fugitive summer twilight still flickered from the garden—I pondered on the awesome loneliness of being my grandfather's age—the loneliness (can you conceive it?) of having *no* contemporaries. And I took stock of the fact that seldom, if ever, had I seen my grandfather—this man of guarded and scrupulous mien—roused by such passion. Only once, indeed, did I see him so roused again—that day of his death, when, despite my efforts to dissuade him, he strode out into the gathering storm.

The sins of my father? What was my father's sin but to seek some other means of outwitting Time than that held out to him? The means of adventure, of hazard and daring, the means of a short life but a full, a memorable one. Was he really impelled by motives so different from those of his own father and his father's father?

Perhaps every third generation is a misfit. Born in 1895, my father would have become the third beneficiary of the Great Watch. From the earliest age, like every true Krepski male-child, he was reared on the staple diet of clocks and chronometry. But, even as a boy, he showed distinct and sometimes hysterical signs of not wishing to assume the family mantle. Grandfather Feliks has told me that he sometimes feared that little Stefan actually plotted to steal the Watch (which he ought to have regarded as the Gift of Gifts) in order to smash it or hide it or simply hurl it away somewhere. My grandfather consequently kept it always on his person and even wore it about his neck, on a locked chain at night—which cannot have aided his sleep.

These were times of great anguish. Stefan was growing up into one of those psychopathic children who wish to wreak merciless destruction on all that their fathers hold dearest. His revolt, unprecedented in the family annals, may seem inexplicable. But I think I understand it. When Feliks was born, his own father Stanislaw was forty: an unexceptional state of affairs. When Stefan grew out of mindless infancy, his father was approaching his first hundred. Who can say how a ten year old reacts to a centenarian father?

And what was Stefan's final solution to paternal oppression? It was a well-tried one, even a hackneyed one, but one never attempted before in our family from land-locked Lublin. At the age of fifteen, in 1910, he ran away to sea, to the beckoning embraces of risk, fortune, fame—or oblivion. It was thought that no more would be seen of him. But this intrepid father of mine, not content with his runaway defiance or with braving the rough world he had pitched himself into, returned, after three years, for the pleasure of staring fixedly into my grandfather's face. He was then a youth of eighteen. But three years' voyaging—to Shanghai, Yokohama, Valparaiso . . .—had toughened his skin and packed into his young frame more resourcefulness than my hundred-year-old grandfather had ever known, bent over his cogs and pendula.

My grandfather realised that he faced a man. That weather-beaten stare was a match for his hundred nominal years. The result of this sailor's return was a reconciliation, a rare balance between father and son—enhanced rather than marred by the fact that only a month or so afterwards Stefan took up with a woman of dubious character—the widow of a music-hall manager (perhaps it is significant that she was twelve years *older* than my father)—got her with child and married her. Thus I arrived on the scene.

My grandfather showed remarkable forbearance. He even stooped for a while to taste the transitory delights of variety artists and buxom singers. It seemed that he would not object—whether it was fitting or not—to Stefan and his lineage partaking of the Watch. It was even possible that Stefan—the only Krepski not to have done so in the way that fish take to swimming and birds to flight—might come round at last to the trade of clock-making.

But all this was not to be. In 1914—the year of my birth—Stefan once more took to the sea, this time in the service of his country (for he was the first Krepski to be born on British soil). Once more there were heated confrontations, but my grandfather could not prevail. Perhaps he knew that even without the pretext of war Stefan would have sooner or later felt stirred again by the life of daring and adventure. Feliks, at last swallowing his anger and disappointment before the parting warrior, held out the prospect of the Watch as a father to a son, even if he could not hold it out as a master clockmaker to a faithful apprentice. Perhaps Stefan might indeed have returned in 1918, a salty hero, ready to settle down and receive its benison. Perhaps he too might have lived to a ripe one hundred, and another hundred more—were it not for the German shell which sent him and the rest of his gallant ship's crew to the bottom at the battle of Jutland.

So it was that I, who knew so intimately my grandfather whose own memories stretched back to Napoleonic times, and would doubtless have known—were it not for that fool of an omnibus driver—my great-grandfather, born while America was still a British colony, have no memories of my father at all. For when the great guns were booming at Jutland and my father's ship was raising its churning propellors to the sky, I was asleep in my cot in Bethnal Green, watched over by my equally unwitting mother. She was to die too, but six months later, of a mixture of grief and influenza. And I passed, at the age of two, into my grandfather's hands, and so into the ghostly hands of my venerable ancestors. From merest infancy I was destined to be a clockmaker, one of the solemn priesthood of Time, and whenever I erred in my noviceship, as on that beguiling evening in Highgate, to have set before me the warning example of my father—dead (though his name lives in glory—you will see it on the memorial at Chatham, the only Krepski amongst all those Jones and Wilsons) at the laughable age of twenty-one.

But this is not a story about my father, nor even about clockmaking. All these lengthy preliminaries are only a way of explaining how on a certain day, a week ago, in a room on the second floor of a delapidated but (as shall be seen) illustrious Victorian building, I, Adam Krepski, sat, pressing in my hand till the sweat oozed from my palm, the Watch made by my great-grandfather, which for over one hundred and seventy years had neither stopped nor ever been wound. The day, as it happens, was my wedding anniversary. A cause for remembrance; but not for celebration. It is nearly thirty years since my wife left me.

And what was making me clutch so tightly that precious mechanism?

It was the cries. The cries coming up the dismal, echoing staircase; the cries from the room on the landing below, which for several weeks I had heard at sporadic intervals, but which now had reached a new, intense note and came with ever-increasing frequency. The cries of a woman, feline, inarticulate—at least to my ears, for I knew them to be the cries of an Asian woman—an Indian, a Pakistani—expressive first of outrage and grief (they had been mixed in those first days with the shouts of a man), but now of pain, of terror, of—it was this that tightened my grip so fervently on that Watch—of unmistakable *urgency*.

My wedding anniversary. Now I consider it, time has played more than one trick on me...

And what was I doing in that gloomy and half-derelict building, I, a Krepski clockmaker? That is a long and ravelled tale—one which begins perhaps on that fateful day in July, 1957, when I married.

My grandfather (who in that same year reached one hundred and fifty) was against it from the outset. The eve of my wedding was another of those humbling moments in my life when he invoked the folly of my father. Not that Deborah had any of the questionable credentials of the widow of a music-hall manager. She was a thirty-five-year-old primary school teacher, and I, after all, was forty-three. But—now my grandfather was midway through his second century—the misogynist bent of our family had reached in him a heightened, indiscriminate pitch. On the death of his third wife, in 1948, he had ceased to play the hypocrite and got himself a housekeeper, not a fourth wife. The disadvantage of this decision, so he sometimes complained to me, was that housekeepers had to be paid. His position towards womankind was entrenched. He saw my marriage-to-be as a hopeless backsliding into the mire of vain biological yearnings and the fraudulent permanence of procreation.

He was wrong. I did not marry to beget children (that fact was to be my undoing) nor to sell my soul to Time. I married simply to have another human being to talk to other than my grandfather.

Do not mistake me. I did not wish to abandon him. I had no intention of giving up my place beside him in the Krepski workshop or of forfeiting my share in the Watch. But consider the weight of his hundred and fifty years on my forty-odd. Consider that since the age of three, not having known my father and, barely, my mother, I had been brought up by this prodigy who even at my birth was over a hundred. Might I feel, in watered-down form, the oppressions and frustrations of my father? At twenty-five I had already grown tired of my grandfather's somehow hollow accounts of the Polish uprisings of 1830, of exiled life in Paris, of the London of the 1850s and '60s. I had begun to perceive that mixed with his blatant misogyny was a more general, brooding misanthropy—a contempt for the common run of men who lived out their meagre three score and ten. His eyes (one of which was permanently out of true from the constant use of a clockmaker's eye-piece) had developed a dull, sanctimonious stare. About his person there hung, like some sick-room smell infesting his clothes, an air of stagnancy, ill-humour, isolation, and even, to judge from his frayed jackets and the disrepair of his Highgate home—relative penury.

For what had become of "Krepski and Krepski, Clock and Watchmakers of Repute," in the course of my lifetime? It was no longer the thriving East End workshop, employing six skilled craftsmen and three apprentices, it had been at the turn of the century. Economic changes had dealt it blows. The mass production of wrist-watches which were now two-a-penny and cheap electrical (electrical!) clocks had squeezed out the small business. On top of this was my grandfather's ever-increasing suspiciousness of nature. For, even if lack of money had not forced him to do so, he would have gradually dismissed his faithful workmen for fear they might discover the secret of the Watch and betray it to the world. That watch could prolong human life but not the life of commercial enterprise. By the 1950s Krepski and Krepski was no more than one of those grimy, tiny, Dickensian-looking shops one can still see on the fringes of the City, sign-boarded "Watch and Clock Repairers" but looking more like a run-down pawnbroker's—to which aged customers would, very occasionally, bring the odd ancient mechanism for a "seeing to."

Grandfather was a hundred and fifty. He looked like a sour-minded but able-bodied man of half that age. Had he retired at the customary time (that is, some time during the 1860s or '70s) he would have known the satisfaction of passing on a business at the peak of its success and of enjoying a comfortable "old age." In the 1950s, still a fit man, he had no choice but to continue at the grinding task of scraping a living. Even had he retired and I had managed to support him, he would have returned, surely enough, to the shop on Goswell Road, like a dog to its kennel.

Imagine the companionship of this man—in our poky, draughty place of work which vibrated ceaselessly to the rumblings of the City traffic outside; in the Highgate house with its flaking paintwork, damp walls and cracked crockery, and only the growlings of Mrs. Murdoch, the housekeeper, to break the monotony. Was I to be blamed for flying with relief from this emtombment to the arms of an impulsive, bright-minded, plumply attractive schoolteacher who—at thirty-five—was actually perturbed by the way the years were passing her by?

• • •

Ah, but in that last fact lay the seeds of marital catastrophe. Grandfather was right. A true Krepski, a true guardian of the Watch, should marry, if he is to marry at all, a plain, stupid and barren wife. Deborah was none of these things: She was that volatile phenomenon, a woman at what for women is a dangerous age, suddenly blessed with the prospect of womanhood fulfilled. Shall I describe our union as merely connubial? Shall I offer the picture of myself as the sober, steady, semi-paternal figure (I was eight years her elder) taking under my sheltering wing this slightly delicate, slightly frightened creature? No. Those first months were a whirlwind, a vortex into which I was sucked, gently at first and then with accelerating and uninhibited voracity. The walls of our first floor flat shook to the onslaughts of female passion; they echoed to Deborah's screams (for at the height of ecstasy Deborah would scream, at an ear-splitting pitch). And I, an, at first, unwitting and passive instrument to all this, a clay figure into which life was rapidly pummeled and breathed, suddenly woke to the fact that for thirty years my life had been measured by clocks; that for people who are not Krepskis, Time is not a servant but an old and pitiless adversary. They have only so long on this earth and they want only to live, to have lived. And when the opportunity comes it is seized with predatory fury.

Deborah, how easy the choice might have been if I had not been a Krepski. Sometimes, in those early days, I would wake up, nestled by my wife's ever-willing flesh and those years in Goswell Road would seem eclipsed: I was once more a boy—as on that audacious summer evening in Highgate—seduced by the world's caress. But then, in an instant,I would remember my grandfather, waiting already at his work-bench, the Great Watch ticking in his pocket, the clock-making, time-enslaving blood that flowed in his and my veins.

How easy the choice if passion were boundless and endless. But it is not, that is the rub; it must be preserved before it perishes and put in some permanent form. All men must make their pact with history. The spring-tide of marriage ebbs, we are told, takes on slower, saner, more effectual rhythms; the white-heat cools, diffuses, but is not lost. All this is natural, and has its natural and rightful object. But it was here that Deborah and I came to the dividing of the ways. I watched my wife through the rusting iron railings of the playground of the primary school where sometimes I met her at lunch-time. There was a delicate, wholesome bloom on her cheeks. Who would have guessed where that bloom came from? Who could have imagined what wild abandon could seize this eminently respectable figure behind closed doors and drawn curtains?

Yet that abandon was no longer indulged; it was withheld, denied (I had come to relish it) and would only be offered freely again in exchange for a more lasting gift. And who could mistake what that gift must be, watching her in the playground, her teacher's whistle round her neck, in the midst of those squealing infants, fully aware that my eyes were on her; patting on the head, as though to make the point unmistakable, now a pugnacious boy with grazed knees, now a Jamaican girl with pigtails?

Had I told her, in all this time, about the Great Watch? Had I told her that I might outlive her by perhaps a century and that our life together—all in all to her—might become (so, alas, it has) a mere oasis in the sands of memory? Had I told her that my grandfather, whom she thought a doughty man of seventy-five, was really twice that age? And had I told her that in us Krepskis the spirit of fatherhood is dead? We do not need children to carry our image into the future, to provide us with that overused bulwark against extinction.

No. I had told her none of these things. I held my tongue in the vain—the wishful?—belief that I might pass in her eyes for an ordinary mortal. If I told her, I assured myself, would she not think I was mad? And, then again, why should I not (was it so great a thing?) flout the scruples which were part of my heritage and give a child to this woman with whom, for a brief period at least, I had explored the timeless realm of passion?

Our marriage entered its fourth year. She approached the ominous age of forty. I was forty-seven, a point at which other men might recognise the signs of age but at which I felt only the protective armour of the Watch tighten around me, the immunity of Krepskihood squeeze me like an iron maiden. Dear Father Stefan, I prayed in hope. But no answering voice came from the cold depths of the Skaggerak or the Heligoland Bight. Instead I imagined a ghostly sigh from far off Poland—and an angry murmuring, perhaps, closer to hand, as Great-grandfather Stanislaw turned in his Highgate grave.

And I looked each day into the tacitly retributive eyes of my grandfather.

Deborah and I waged war. We bickered, we quarrelled, we made threats. And then at last, abandoning all subterfuge, I told her.

She did not think I was mad. Something in my voice, my manner told her that this was not madness. If it had been madness, perhaps, it would have been easier to endure. Her face turned white. In one fell stroke her universe was upturned. Her stock of love, her hungry flesh, her empty womb were mocked and belittled. She looked at me as if I might have been a monster with two heads or a fish's tail. The next day she fled—"left me" is too mild a term—and, rather than co-exist another hour with my indefinite lease on life, returned to her mother, who—poor soul—was ailing, in need of nursing, and shortly to die.

Tick-tock, tick-tock. The invalid clocks clanked and wheezed on the shelves in Goswell Road. Grandfather showed tact. He did not rub salt in the wound. Our reunion even had, too, its brief honeymoon. The night of Deborah's departure I sat up with him in the house at Highgate and he recalled, not with the usual dry deliberateness but with tender spontaneity, the lost Poland of his youth. Yet this very tenderness was an ill omen. Men of fantastic age are not given to nostalgia. It is the brevity of life, the rapid passage of finite years, that gives rise to sentiment and regret. During my interlude with Deborah a change had crept over my grandfather. The air of stagnancy, the fixation in the eyes were still there but what was new was that he himself seemed aware of these things as he had not before. Sorrow shadowed his face, and weariness, weariness.

The shop was on its last legs. Anyone could see there was no future in it; and yet for Grandfather, for me, there was, always, future. We pottered away, in the musty workroom, eking out what scant business came our way. The Great Watch, that symbol of Time conquered ticking remorselessly in Grandfather's waistcoat, had become, we knew, our master. Sometimes I dreamt wildly of destroying it, of taking a hammer to its invulnerable mechanism. But how could I have committed an act so sacrilegious, and one which, for all I knew, might have reduced my grandfather, in an instant to dust?

We worked on. I remember the hollow mood—neither relief nor reluctance but some empty reflex between the two—with which we shut the shop each night at six and made our journey home. How we would sit, like two creatures sealed in a bubble, as our number 43 trundled up the Holloway Road, watching the fretfulness of the evening rush (how frenzied the activity of others when one's own pace is slow and interminable) with a cold reptilean stare.

Ah, happy restless world, with oblivion waiting to solve its cares.

Ah, lost Deborah, placing gladioli on the grave of her mother.

The sons, and grandsons, of the ordinary world do their duty by their sires. They look after them in their twilight years. But what if twilight never falls?

By the summer of my grandfather's hundred and sixty-second year I could endure no more. With the last dregs of my feeble savings I rented a cottage in the Sussex downs. My aim was to do what necessity urged: to sell up the shop; to find myself a job with a steady income by which I might support Grandfather and myself. Admittedly, I was now fifty-five, but my knowledge of clocks might find me a place with an antique dealer's or as sub-curator in some obscure museum of horology. In order to attempt all this, Grandfather had first to be lured to a safe distance.

This is not to say that the cottage was merely an—expensive—expedient. One part of me sincerely wished my grandfather to stop peering into the dusty orbs of clocks and to peer out again at the World—even the tame, parochial world of Sussex. Ever lurking in my mind was the notion that age ripens, mellows and brings it own, placid contentments. Why had not his unique length of years afforded my grandfather more opportunity to enjoy, to savour, to contemplate the world? Why should he not enter now an era of meditative tranquillity, of god-like congruence with Nature? Youth should bow to age not only in duty but in veneration. Perhaps I had always been ashamed—perhaps it was a source of secret despair for my own future—that my grandfather's years had only produced in him the crabbed, cantankerous creature I knew. Perhaps I hoped that extraordinary age might have instilled in him extraordinary sagacity. Perhaps I saw him—wild, impossible vision—turning in his country hermitage into some hallowed figure, a Sussex shaman, a Wise Man of the Downs, an oracle to whom the young and foolish world might flock for succour.

Or perhaps my motive was simpler than this. Perhaps it was no more than that of those plausible, burdened sons and daughters who, with well-meaning looks and at no small cost, place their parents in Homes, in order to have them out of sight and mind—in order, that is, to have them safely murdered.

My clinching argument was that, though all that would be left of Krepski and Krepski would be the Great Watch, yet that all would be all-in-all. And as a preliminary concession I agreed to spend a first experimental weekend with him at the cottage.

• • •

We travelled down on a Friday afternoon. It was one of those close, sullen high-summer days which make the flesh crawl and seem to bring out from nowhere swarms of flying insects. Grandfather sat in his seat in the railway carriage and hid his face behind a newspaper. This, like the weather, was a bad sign. Normally, he regarded papers with disdain. What did the news of 1977 mean to a man born in 1808? Almost by definition, papers were tokens of man's subjection to time; their business was ephemerality. Yet recently, so I had noticed, he had begun to buy them and to read them almost with avidity; and what his eyes went to first were reports of accidents and disasters, sudden violent deaths...

Now and then, as we passed through the Surrey suburbs, he came out from behind his screen. His face was not the face of a man travelling towards rejuvenating horizons. It was the petrified face of a man whom no novelty can touch.

The Sussex downs, an hour from London, still retain their quiet nooks and folds. Our cottage—one of a pair let by some palm-rubbing local speculator as weekend retreats—stood at one end of the village and at the foot of one of these characteristic, peculiarly female eminences of the Downs, referred to in the Ordnance Survey map as a beacon. In spite of the sticky heat, I proposed this as the object of a walk the day after our arrival. The place was a noted viewpoint. Let us look down, I thought, us immortals, at the world.

Grandfather was less enthusiastic. His reluctance had nothing to do with his strength of limb. The climb was steep, but Grandfather despite his years, was as fit as a man of forty. His unwillingness lay in a scarcely concealed desire to sabotage and deride this enterprise of mine. He had spent the first hours after our arrival shambling around the cottage, not bothering to unpack his things, inspecting the oak timbers, the "traditional fireplace" and the "charming cottage garden" with an air of acid distaste, and finally settling heavily into a chair in just the same hunched manner in which he settled into his habitual chair in Highgate or his work stool at the shop. Long life ought to elicit a capacity for change. But it is the opposite (I know it well). Longevity encourages intransigence, conservatism. It teaches you to revert to type.

The sultry weather had not freshened. Half way up the slope of the beacon we gave up our ascent, both of us in a muck-sweat. Even at this relative height no breezes challenged the leaden atmosphere, and the famous view, northwards to the Weald of Kent, was lost in grey curtains of haze and the shadows of black, greasy clouds. We sat on the tussocked grass, recovering our breath, Grandfather a little to one side and below me, mute as boulders. The silence hanging between us was like an epitaph upon my futile hopes: Give up this doomed exercise.

And yet, not silence. That is, not *our* silence—but the silence in which we sat. A silence which, as our gasps for breath subsided, became gradually palpable, audible, insistent. We sat, listening, on the warm grass, ears pricked like alert rabbits. We forgot our abortive climb. When had we last heard such silence, used as we were to the throbbing traffic of the Goswell Road? And what a full, what a tumultuous silence. Under the humid pressure of the atmosphere the earth was opening up its pores and the silence was a compound of its numberless exhalations. The downs themselves—those great feminine curves of flesh—were tingling, oozing. And what were all the components of this massive silence—the furious hatching of insects, the sighing of the grass, the trill of larks, the far-off bleat of sheep—but the issue of that swelling pregnancy? What, in turn, was that pregnancy, pressing, even as we sat, into our puny backsides, but the pregnancy of Time?

Old, they say, as the hills. Grandfather sat motionless, his face turned away from me. For a moment, I imagined the tough, chalk-scented grass spreading over him, rising round him to make of him no more than a turf cairn. On the Ordnance Survey maps were the acne-marks of neolithic barrows and Iron Age earthworks.

Silence. And the only noise, the only man-made obtrusion into that overpowering silence was the tick of Great-grandfather's Watch.

We began to descend. Grandfather's face wore a look of gloom; of humility, of pride, of remorse, contrition—despair.

The night was quick in coming, hastened by the louring clouds. And it brought the appropriate conditions—a drop in temperature, a clash of air currents—to release the pent up explosion. As the electricity in the atmosphere accumulated, so Grandfather grew increasingly restless. He began to pace about the cottage, face twitching, darting black scowls in my direction. Twice, he got out the Watch, looked at it as if on the verge of some dreadful decision, then with an agonised expression returned it to his pocket. I was afraid of him. Thunder clattered and lightning flashed in the distance. And then, as if an invisible giant had taken a vast stride, a wind tore at the elm trees in the lane, half a dozen unfamiliar doors and windows banged in the cottage, and the bolts from heaven seemed suddenly aimed at a point over our heads. Grandfather's agitation intensified accordingly. His lips worked at themselves. I expected them to froth. Another whirlwind outside. I went upstairs to fasten one of the banging windows. When I returned he was standing by the front door, buttoning his raincoat.

"Don't try to stop me!"

But I could not have stopped him if I had dared. His mania cast an uncrossable barrier around him. I watched him pass out into the frenzied air. Barely half a minute after his exit the skies opened and rain lashed down.

I was not so obtuse as to imagine that my grandfather had gone for a mere stroll. But something kept me from pursuing him. I sat in a rocking chair by the "traditional fireplace," waiting and (discern my motive if you will) even smiling, fixedly, while the thunder volleyed outside. Something about the drama of the moment, something about this invasion of the elements into our lives I could not help but find (like the man who grins idiotically at his executioner) gratifying.

And then I acted. The beacon: that was the best place for storm watching. For defying—or inviting—the wrath of the skies. I reached for my own waterproof and walking shoes and strode out into the tumult.

During a thunder-storm, in Thuringia, so the story goes, Martin Luther broke down, fell to his knees, begged the Almighty for forgiveness and swore to become a monk. I am not a religious man—had I not been brought up to regard a certain timepiece as the only object of worship?—but that night I feared for my soul; that night I believe a God was at work, directing my steps to the scene of divine revenge. The thunder beat its drum. By the intermittent flashes of lightning I found my way to the slopes of the beacon; but, once there, it seemed I did not need a guide to point my course—I did not need to reach the top and stand there like some demented weathercock. The downs are bald, bold formations and in the magnesium-glare of lightning any features could be picked out. Clinging to the incline was a solitary clump of trees, of the kind which, on the downs, are said to have a druidical significance. I needed to go no further. One of the trees had been split and felled by a scimitar of lightning. Grandfather lay lifeless beside its twisted wreckage, an anguished grimace frozen on his face. And in his waistcoat pocket, beneath his sodden coat and jacket, the Great Watch, its tiny, perfect, mechanical brain ignorant of storms, of drama, of human catastrophe, still ticked indifferently.

Help me, powers that be! Help me, Father Time! I stood in the crematorium, the last of the Krepskis, the Great Watch ticking in my pocket. Flames completed on Grandfather the work of the lightning, and reduced, in a matter of seconds, his one-hundred-

and-sixty-year-old body to cinders. That day, a day so different—a tranquil, golden August day—from that night of death, I could have walked away and become a new man. I could have traced my steps—only a short distance—to the school playground where Deborah still stood among her frolicking brood, and asked to be reconciled. Her mother; my grandfather. The chastening bonds of bereavement.

I could have flung the Watch away. Indeed, I considered having it incinerated with Grandfather's corpse—but the rules of crematoria are strict on such matters. And did I not, that same afternoon, having attended the perfunctory reading of a barren will at a solicitor's in Chancery Lane, walk on the Thames Embankment, under the plane trees, holding the Watch in my sweating hand and daring myself to throw it? Twice I drew back my arm and twice let it fall. From the glinting river the waterborne voice of my father said, Why not? Why not? But I thought of Grandfather's ashes, still warm and active in their urn (surely when one lives the best part of two centuries one does not die so quickly?). I thought of Great-grandfather Stanislaw, and of his forebears, whose names I knew like a litany—Stanislaw senior, Kasimierz, Ignacy, Tadeusz. In the curving reaches of the Thames I saw what I had never seen: the baroque spires of Lublin; the outstretched plains of Poland.

It is true what the psychologists say: Our ancestors are our first and only gods. It is from them we get our guilt, our duty, our sin—our destiny. A few claps of thunder had awed me, a few celestial firecrackers had given me a passing scare. I gripped the Watch. I did not go back to the infants' school that afternoon, nor even, at first, to the house in Highgate. I went—all the way on foot, like a devout pilgram—to the street in Whitechapel where my great-grandfather, a flourishing clockmaker in his hundred and twelfth year had set up a home in the 1870s. In the 1870s there were fine houses as well as slums in Whitechapel. The street was still there. And so was the old home—its crumbling stucco, its cracked and boarded-up windows, its litter-strewn front steps a mockery of the former building which had once boasted two maids and a cook. I stared at it. By some prompting of fate, by some inevitable reflex on my part, I knocked on the door. The face of an Asian woman; timid, soulful. Someone had told me there was a room to let in this house. Yes, it was true—on the second floor.

So I did not throw away the Watch: I found a shrine in which to place it. And I did not return—save to dispose of its meagre contents and arrange its sale—to the house in Highgate. I re-fashioned my world, on a hermit's terms, out of an ancestral room in Whitechapel. Time, as even the ignorant will tell you and every clock-face will demonstrate, is circular. The longer you live, the more you long to go back, to go back. I closed my eyes on that old charlatan, the future. And Deborah remained for ever in her playground, whistling at her children, like some-one vainly whistling for a runaway dog which already lies dead at the side of a road.

Thus I came to be sitting, a week ago, in that same room in Whitechapel, clutching, as I had that day by the Thames, the Watch in my itching palm. And still they came, the cries, desolate and unappeasable, from the floor below.

What was the meaning of these cries? I knew (I who had renounced such things to live in perpetual marriage with the Watch) they were the cries that come from the interminglings of men and women, the cries of heart-break and vain desire. I knew they were the cries of that same Asian woman who had opened the door for me that day of Grandfather's cremation. A Mrs.—or Miss?—Matharu. The husband (lover?) had come and gone at varying times. A shift-worker of some sort. Sometimes I met him on the stairs. An exchange of nods; a word. But I did not seek more. I burrowed in my ancestral lair. And even when the shouting began—his ferocious, rapid, hers like some ruffled, clucking bird—I did not intervene. Thunder-storms pass. Clocks tick on. The shouts were followed by screams, blows, the noise of slamming doors—sobs. Still I sat tight. Then one day the door slammed with the unmistakable tone of finality (ah, Deborah); and the sobs that followed were not the sobs that still beg and plead, but solitary sobs, whimpering and dirge-like—the sobs of the lonely lingering out the empty hours.

Did I go down the stairs. Did I give a gentle knock to the door and ask softly, "Can I help?" No. The world is full of snares.

Time heals. Soon these whimperings would cease. And so they did. Or, rather, faded into almost-silence—only to build up again into new crescendos of anguish.

I gripped my ticking talisman, as the sick and dying cling, in their hour of need, to pitiful trinkets. Do not imagine that these female cries merely assailed my peace and did not bring to me, as to their utterer, real suffering. I recognised that they emanated from a region ungoverned by time—and thus were as poisonous, as lethal to us Krepskis as fresh air to a fish.

We were alone in the building, this wailing woman and I. The house—the whole street—lay under the ultimatum of a compulsory purchase. The notices had been issued. Already the other rooms were vacated. And already, beyond my windows, walls were tumbling, bulldozers were sending clouds of dust into the air. The house of Krepski must fall soon; as had fallen already the one-time houses of Jewish tailors, Dutch goldsmiths, Russian furriers—a whole neighborhood of immigrant tradesmen, stepping off the ships at London docks and bringing with them the strands of their far-flung pasts. How could it be that all this history had been reduced, before my eyes, to a few heaps of flattened rubble and a few grey demarcations of corrugated fencing?

Another rending cry, like the tearing of flesh itself. I stood up: I clutched my forehead; sat down; stood up again. I descended the stairs. But I did not loosen my grip on the Watch.

She lay—beneath a tangled heap of bedclothes, on a mattress in the large, draughty room which I imagined had once been my great-grandfather's drawing-room, but which now served as living-room, kitchen and bedroom combined—in the obvious grip not so much of grief as of illness. Clearly, she had been unable to answer my knock at the door, which was unlocked, and perhaps had been for weeks. Sweat beaded her face. Her eyes burned. And even as I stood over her she drew a constricted gasp of pain and her body shuddered beneath the heaped bedclothes which I suspected had been pulled rapidly about her as I entered.

Circumstances conspire. This woman, as I knew from the dozen words we had exchanged in little more than a year, spoke scarcely any English. She could not describe her plight; I could not inquire. No language was needed to tell me I should fetch a doctor, but as I bent over her, with the caution with which any Krepski bends over a woman, she suddenly gripped my arm, no less fiercely than my free hand gripped the Watch. When I signalled my intention, mouthing the word "doctor" several times, she gripped it tightly still, and an extra dimension of torment seemed to enter her face. It struck me that had I been a younger man (I was sixty-three, but little did she know that in Krepski terms I was still callow) her grip on my arm might have been less ready. Even so, fear as much as importunacy knotted her face. More than one layer of shame seemed present in her eyes as she let out another uncontrollable moan and her body strained beneath the bedclothes.

"What's wrong? What's wrong?"

You will doubtless think me foolish and colossally ignorant for not recognising before this point the symptoms of child-birth. For such they were. I, a Krepski who held in my hand the power to live so long and whose forefathers had lived so long before him, did not recognise the beginnings of life, and did not know what a woman in labour is like. But, once the knowledge dawned, I understood not only the fact but its implications and the reasons for this woman's mingled terror and entreaty. The child was the child of a fugitive father. Daddy was far away, ignorant perhaps of this fruit of his dalliance, just as my father Stefan, far away on the North Sea, was ignorant of my mother stooping over my cot. Daddy, perhaps, was no Daddy by law; and who could say whether by *law* either Daddy or Mummy were rightful immigrants? That might explain the hand gripping me so tightly as I turned for professional help. Add to all this that I was an Englishman and I bent over this woman—whose mother had perhaps worn a veil in some village by the Ganges—as she suffered the most intimate female distress... You will see the position was vexed.

And I had no choice but to be the witness—the midwife—to this hopeless issue.

I understood that the moment was near. Her black-olive eyes fixed me from above the tangled sheets, in which, as if obeying some ancient instinct, she tried to hide her mouth. The point must soon come when she must abandon all modesty—and I all squeamishness—and I could see her weighing this terrible candour against the fact that I was her only help.

But as we stared at each other a strange thing happened. In the little half-oval of face which she showed me I seemed to see, as if her eyes were equipped with some extraordinary ultra-optical lens, the huge hinterlands of her native Asia and the endless nut-brown faces of her ancestors. At the same time, marshalled within myself, assembling from the distant margins of Poland, were the ranks of my Krepski sires. What a strange thing that our lives should collide, here where neither had its origins. How strange that they should collide at all. What a strange and extraordinary thing that I should be born a Krepski, she a Matharu. What an impossible concatenation of chances goes to the making of any birth.

I must have smiled at these thoughts—or at least lent to my

face some expression which infected hers. For her look suddenly softened—her black irises melted—then immediately hardened again. She screwed her eyes shut, let out a scream, and with a gesture of submission—as she might have submitted to that brute of a husband—pulled back the bedclothes from the lower part of her body, drew up her legs, and, clutching at the bed-head, with her hands, began to strain mightily.

Her eyes were shut; I think they remained shut throughout the whole ensuing procedure. But mine opened, wider and wider, at what perhaps no Krepski had seen, or at least *viewed* with such privileged and terrified intentness. The mother—for this is what she was now indubitably becoming—arched her spine, heaved her monstrous belly, seemed to offer her whole body to be cleaved from between the legs upwards, and those expanding eyes of mine saw a glistening, wet, purple-mottled object, like some wrinkled marble pebble, appear where the split began. This pebble grew—and grew—growing impossibly large for the narrow opening in which it seemed intent on jamming itself. For a whole minute, indeed, it stuck there, as if this were its final resting place, while the mother screamed. And then suddenly it ceased to be a pebble. It was a lump of clenched, unformed flesh, suffused with blood, aware that its position was critical. The mother gasped; it became a head, a gnarled, battered, Punch-and-Judy head. The mother gasped again, this time with an audible relief and exultation; and it was no longer a head, but a whole *creature*, with arms and legs and little groping hands; and it was no longer caught in that awesome constriction but suddenly spilling out with slippery ease, like something poured from a pickle jar, a slithery brine accompanying it. But this was not all. As if it were not remarkable enough that so large a thing should emerge from so small a hole, there followed it, rapidly, an indescribable mass of multicoloured effluents, the texture and hue of liquid coral, gelatine, stewed blackberries...

From what a ragout is a human life concocted.

What was I doing throughout this spectacular performance? My eyes were popping, my knees were giving. I was clutching the Great Watch, fit to crush it, in my right hand. But now, with the little being writhing in slow motion on the gory sheets and the mother's moans of relief beginning to mingle with a new anguish, I knew that I had my own unavoidable part to play in this drama. Once, on Grandfather's television at Highgate, I had watched (disgusted but fascinated) a programme about child-delivery. I knew that much pertained to the fleshy tube which even now snaked and coiled between mother and baby. The mother understood it too; for with her last reserves of energy she was gesturing to a chest of drawers on the fair side of the room. In one of the drawers I found a pair of kitchen scissors . . .

With the instant of birth begins the possibility of manslaughter. My untutored hands did what they could while my stomach fought down surging tides—not just of nausea but of strange, welling fear. Like the TV surgeon, I held up the slippery creature and, with an irresolute hand, slapped it. It grimaced feebly and made the sound—a sound of choking pain—which they say means life has taken hold. But it looked wretched and sick to me. I put it down on the mattress close to the mother's side, as if some maternal fluence could do the trick I could not. We looked at each other, she and I, with the imploring looks of actual lovers, actual cogenitors who have pooled their flesh in a single hope.

Deborah . . . with your playground whistle.

I had heard the expression "life hangs in the balance." I knew that it applied to tense moments in operating theatres and in condemned cells when a reprieve may still come, but I never knew—used to life as an ambling affair that might span centuries—what it meant. And only now do I know what enormous concentrations of time, what huge counter-forces of piled-up years, decades, centuries, go into those moments when the balance might swing, one way or the other.

We looked at the pitiful child. Its blind face was creased; its fingers worked. Its breaths were clearly numbered. The mother began to blubber, adding yet more drops to her other, nameless outpourings; and I felt my ticking, clockmaker's heart swell inside me. A silent, involuntary prayer escaped me.

And suddenly they were there again. Stanislaw and Feliks and Stefan; winging towards me by some uncanny process, bringing with them the mysterious essence of the elements that had received them and decomposed them. Great-grandfather from his Highgate grave, Grandfather from his urn, Father (was he the first to arrive?) from the grey depths where the fishes had nibbled him and the currents long since corroded and dispersed him. Earth, fire, water. They flocked out of the bowels of Nature. And with them came Stanislaw senior, Kasimierz, Tadeusz; and all the others whose names I forget; and even the mythical Krepfs of Nuremberg and Prague.

My hand was on the magic, genie-summoning Watch. In that moment I knew that Time is not something that exists, like territory to be annexed, outside us. What are we all but the distillation of all time? What is each one of us but the sum of all the time before him?

The little baby chest was trembling feebly; the hands still groped; the wrinkled face was turning blue. I held out the Great Watch of Stanislaw. I let it swing gently on its gold chain over the miniscule fingers of this new-born child. They say the first instinct a baby has is to grasp. It touched the ticking masterpiece fashioned in Lublin in the days of the Grand Duchy of Warsaw. A tiny forefinger and thumb clasped with the force of feathers the delicately chased gold casing and the thick, yellowed glass. A second—an eternity passed. And then—the almost motionless chest began to heave vigorously. The face knotted itself up to emit a harsh, stuttering wail, in the timbre of which there seemed the rudiments of a chuckle. The mother's tearful eyes brightened. At the same time I felt inside me a renewed flutter of fear. No, not of fear exactly: a draining away of something; a stripping away of some imposture, as if I had no right to be where I was.

The diminutive fingers still gripped the Watch. Through the gold chain I felt the faintest hint of a baby tug. And a miraculous thing—as miraculous as this infant's resurgence of life—happened. I set it down now as a fact worthy to be engraved in record. At six-thirty P.M. on a July day scarcely a week ago, the hand of a baby (what titanic power must have been in those fingers, what pent-up equivalent of years and years of accumulated time?) stopped my great-grandfather's Watch, which had ticked, without requiring the hand of man to wind it, since September, 1809.

The fear—the sensation of being assailed from within—clutched me more intently. This room, in the house of my great-grandfather—in which my ancestors themselves had invisibly mustered (had they fled already, exorcised ghosts?)—was no longer my sanctuary but the centre of a desert. Weighing upon me with a force to equal that which had kept this child alive, was the desolation of my future, growing older and older, but never old enough, and growing every day, more puny, more shrivelled, more insectile.

I released my grip on the chain. I pressed the Great Watch into the hands of an infant. I got up from my position squatting by the mattress. I looked at the mother. How could I have explained, even if I had her language? The baby was breathing; it would live. The mother would pull through. I knew this better than any doctor. I turned to the door and made my exit. Things grew indistinct around me. I stumbled down the flight of stairs to the street door.

Outside, I found a phone-box and, giving the barest particulars, called an ambulance to the mother and child. Then I blundered on. No, not if you are thinking this, in the direction of Deborah. Nor in the direction of the Thames, to hurl, not the Watch, but myself into the murky stream and join my sea-changed father.

Not in any direction. No direction was necessary. For in the historic streets of Whitechapel, minutes later, I was struck, not by an omnibus, not by an arrow of lighting, nor by a shell from one of the Kaiser's iron-clads, but by an internal blow, mysterious and devasting, a blow by which not physical trees but family trees are toppled and torn up by their roots.

Another ambulance wailed down Stepney Way, not for a mother and child, but for me.

And now *I* lie beneath fevered bedclothes. And now I can tell—from the disinterested if baffled faces of doctors (who no doubt have a different way of gauging time from clockmakers), from the looks of buxom nurses (ah—Deborah) who bend over my bed, lift my limp wrist and eye their regulation-issue watches—that my own breaths are numbered.

ABOUT THE AUTHOR

GRAHAM SWIFT, born in 1949, was nominated as one of the twenty Best of Young British Novelists. He is also the author of three novels, *The Sweet-Shop Owner*, *Shuttlecock*, and *Waterland*.